AUTHOR

COLLINS, W.

CLASS F

TITLE

My lady's money

CLITHEROE

D0226673

MY LADY'S MONEY

WILKIE COLLINS

MY LADY'S MONEY
An Episode in the Life
of a Young Girl

ALAN SUTTON

First published 1879

First published in this edition in the United Kingdom in 1990 by
Alan Sutton Publishing Limited · Phoenix Mill · Far Thrupp
Stroud · Gloucestershire

Copyright © in this edition
Alan Sutton Publishing Limited 1990

British Library Cataloguing in Publication Data

Collins, Wilkie *1824–1889*
  My lady's money: an episode in the life of a young girl.
  I. Title
  823.8 [F]

  ISBN 0–86299–854–X

Cover picture: Afternoon tea *by Elizabeth S. Guinness (fl. 1873–1900).*
(Photograph: Fine Art Photographic Library Limited.)

Typeset in 9/10 Bembo.
Typesetting and origination by
Alan Sutton Publishing Limited.
Printed in Great Britain by
The Guernsey Press Company Limited,
Guernsey, Channel Islands.

CONTENTS

BIOGRAPHICAL NOTE

WILLIAM WILKIE COLLINS was born on 8 January 1824, in New Cavendish Street, London, the elder son of William Collins, a fashionable and successful painter of the early nineteenth century, who counted among his friends Wordsworth and Coleridge. William Collins was a religious man, and in his strict observances may have been a repressive influence on his son, who appears to have inherited his mother Harriet Geddes' attractive and friendly personality. Wilkie was named after his godfather, Sir David Wilkie, RA, a bachelor and close friend of the family.

Little is known of Wilkie's early life. His brother, Charles, was born in 1828, and the family lived comfortably, first in Hampstead, then in Bayswater, where Wilkie attended Maida Hill Academy. The following year the whole family left for Italy, where they spent two years, visiting the major art collections and learning Italian. On their return, Wilkie attended a private boarding school in Highbury, where his story-telling talent was recognized and exploited by a senior prefect who demanded, with the threat of physical violence, to be entertained. 'Thus,' wrote Collins, 'I learnt to be amusing on a short notice and have derived benefit from those early lessons.'

When he left school in 1840, he showed no inclination to enter the Church, as his father wished, and chose, without enthusiasm, the world of commerce, accepting a post with Antrobus & Co., tea importers. He was totally unsuited to the regularity of business life, preferring to escape to the vibrant atmosphere of Paris. He started to write articles and short stories, which were accepted for publication, albeit anonymously, and in 1846 his father agreed that he should leave commerce and take up law, which would, in theory, provide him with a regular income. He studied at Lincoln's Inn Fields, and was finally called to the bar, but his legal knowledge was to be applied creatively in his novels, rather than practically in the law courts.

In his early twenties Collins painted as well as writing. He had many friends who were artists, and he supported the new Pre-Raphaelite movement. In 1848 he had a picture exhibited in the Royal Academy. In the same year his first book was published: the memoirs of his father, who had died the previous year. These were diligently researched and provided a training ground for the emerging writer, developing his thorough methodical approach to compilation and exercising his descriptive ability. His first novel, *Antonia* was published by Bentley's two years later. Although of no great literary merit, it was written in the then popular mode of historical romance, and so enjoyed instant success. The following year Bentley's published *Rambles beyond Railways*, an account of a holiday in Cornwall, which reflected Collins' life-long love of wild and remote places.

It was in the same year, 1851, that Wilkie Collins first met Charles Dickens, an introduction effected by their mutual friend, the artist, Augustus Egg. The meeting was significant for both, leading to a close friendship and working partnership from which both benefited. Dickens had found a friend of more stable temperament than himself, affable and tolerant, responsive to his restless demanding nature. From Collins he acquired the skill of economic and taut plotting, as evidenced in *A Tale of Two Cities* (which may be interestingly compared with Collins' story of the French Revolution, *Sister Rose*, 1855), and in his later novels. Collins was welcomed by the Dickens family, and spent many holidays with them in England and France. He was encouraged and guided in his writing by Dickens, and he must have been stimulated by the latter's enthusiasm and vitality. The two authors worked together on Dickens' magazines, *Household Words*, and *All the Year Round*. Collins was employed as an editor, and many of his works appeared first in these publications, while both writers collaborated on several short stories.

A Terribly Strange Bed – Collins' first work in the macabre genre – was the first of his short stories to appear in *Household Words*, in 1852. The following year the magazine saw the publication of *Gabriel's Marriage*, a story of a Breton fishing community. In the interim, Dickens had turned down *Mad Monkton*, a study of inherited insanity, as unsuitable subject matter, and this was later published by *Fraser's Magazine* in 1855. These two, along with *Sister Rose, The Yellow Mask*, and *A Stolen Letter*, were originally published in *Household Words*, and reprinted in *After Dark*, 1855, for which anthology Collins wrote the successfully economic and melodramatic *Lady of Glenwith Grange* (an inspiration for Miss Haversham?). *A Rogue's Life*, Collins' venture into the picaresque, was serialized in 1856. This was followed in 1857 by *The Dead Secret*, a full length novel, which in its complexity suggests the author's technical potential. *The Biter Bit*, which was published in 1858 and is commonly held to be the first humorous detective story, shows Collins' development of the epistolary form. Both of his two greatest novels, *The Woman in White* and *The Moonstone*, appeared first as serializations in *All the Year Round* – as did the less well known *No Name*. This unconventional study of illegitimacy was published in its full form in 1862, two years after the masterpiece of suspense and drama *The Woman in White* and six years before his original detective story, *The Moonstone*, appeared as complete books.

Another interest shared by Collins and Dickens was a love of the theatre. *The Frozen Deep*, 1857, written by Collins and starring Dickens, was inspired by an interest in the Arctic exploration of the time. It was followed by a series of minor productions, the stage version of *No Thoroughfare* (with combined authorship), enjoying a record run of two hundred nights in 1867.

Anyone meeting Collins in those days would have seen:

A neat figure of a cheerful plumpness, very small feet and hands, a full brown beard, a high and rounded forehead, a small nose not naturally intended to support a pair of large spectacles behind which his eyes shone with humour and friendship.

R.C. Lehmann, *Memories of Half a Century*

But how many would have glimpsed, as did the young artist, Rudolf Lehmann, the strange far-off look in his eyes, which gave the impression of investing 'almost everything with an

air of mystery and romance'? It was suggestive of a depth of
personality not accessible to many, but demonstrated by the
author's expressed unconventional views of the class and
social *mores* of the day; which were further borne out by what
is known of his personal life. During the 1860s, Collins met
and fell in love with Caroline Graves, who had a daughter by a
previous marriage. He never married her, but lived with
mother and daughter for most of the remainder of his life. In
1868, Caroline mysteriously married another, and Collins
entered into a relationship with Martha Judd, by whom he had
three children. However, by the early 1870s, he was once
more living with Caroline, who was still known as Mrs
Graves. It has been suggested that Martha Judd may have been
employed originally by Collins as an amanuensis. Over the
years Collins' health had been deteriorating. He was a victim
of gout, which attacked his whole body, including his eyes.
He suffered a particularly severe attack in 1868, when his
mother died, and he was working on *The Moonstone*. A
dedicated woman, capable of disregarding his suffering and
attending only to his words was employed, to whom Collins
dictated the rest of the work, but she has never been named.

   In 1870 Charles Dickens died. During the previous ten years
Collins had produced his best work: the three novels serialized
in *All the Year Round*; *Armadale*, 1866, in the *Cornhill Magazine*,
and *Man and Wife*, 1870, in *Cassell's Magazine*. But with
Dickens' death, something in Collins seemed to die too,
although his popularity remained undiminished. His novels,
produced regularly until his death, were widely read, and his
was some of the first fiction to appear in cheap editions. In the
1870s he enjoyed some success with the stage versions of his
novels, which were produced both in London and the
provinces. Not only was Collins' work popular in England;
his novels and plays were translated and produced in most
European countries, including Russia, and were widely avail-
able in America. In 1873 Collins was invited to give readings
in the eastern United States and Canada. Although his reading
lacked the vitality of Dickens, the Americans were charmed
by him.

   Of course, it was not only Dickens' death which adversely
affected Collins' work. His gout was becoming persistent, and

he relied increasingly on laudenum to relieve the pain. However, he never lost his mental clarity, taking care to be properly informed about medicine, drugs and chemistry, as is clearly shown in *Heart and Science,* 1883 and the detailed notes he left for his last novel, *Blind Love*, 1890 – completed, posthumously, at his request, by Walter Besant. During his later years, his social life was restricted by poor health, but he did not become a recluse as has been suggested. He maintained close friendships with Charles Reade, Holman Hunt, the Beard and the Lehmann families, and theatrical people, including Ada Cavendish and Mary Anderson. In 1889, after being involved in a cab accident, Collins' health rapidly declined, and he died while suffering from bronchitis on 23 September. He was buried at Kensal Green Cemetery.

SHEILA MICHELL

MY LADY'S MONEY

PERSONS OF THE STORY

WOMEN

LADY LYDIARD (*Widow of Lord Lydiard*)
ISABEL MILLER (*her Adopted Daughter*)
MISS PINK (*of South Morden*)
THE HON. MRS DRUMBLADE (*Sister to the Hon. A. Hardyman*)

MEN

THE HON. ALFRED HARDYMAN (*of the Stud Farm*)
MR FELIX SWEETSIR (*Lady Lydiard's Nephew*)
ROBERT MOODY (*Lady Lydiard's Footman*)
MR TROY (*Lady Lydiard's Lawyer*)
OLD SHARON (*in the Byeways of Legal Bohemia*)

ANIMAL

TOMMIE (*Lady Lydiard's Dog*)

PART THE FIRST

THE DISAPPEARANCE

CHAPTER I

Old Lady Lydiard sat meditating by the fireside, with three letters lying open on her lap.

Time had discoloured the paper, and had turned the ink to a brownish hue. The letters were all addressed to the same person — 'THE RIGHT HON. LORD LYDIARD' — and were all signed in the same way – 'Your affectionate cousin, James Tollmidge.' Judged by these specimens of his correspondence, Mr Tollmidge must have possessed one great merit as a letter-writer – the merit of brevity. He will weary nobody's patience, if he is allowed to have a hearing. Let him, therefore, be permitted, in his own high-flown way, to speak for himself.

First Letter. – 'My statement, as your Lordship requests, shall be short and to the point. I was doing very well as a portrait-painter in the country; and I had a wife and children to consider. Under the circumstances, if I had been left to decide for myself, I should certainly have waited until I had saved a little money before I ventured on the serious expense of taking a house and studio at the west end of London. Your Lordship, I positively declare, encouraged me to try the experiment without waiting. And here I am, unknown and unemployed, a helpless artist lost in London – with a sick wife and hungry children, and bankruptcy staring me in the face. On whose shoulders does this dreadful responsibility rest? On your Lordship's!'

Second Letter. – 'After a week's delay, you favour me, my Lord, with a curt reply. I can be equally curt on my side. I indignantly deny that I or my wife ever presumed to see your Lordship's name as a means of recommendation to sitters

11

without your permission. Some enemy has slandered us. I claim as my right to know the name of that enemy.'

Third (and last) Letter. – 'Another week has passed – and not a word of answer has reached me from your Lordship. It matters little. I have employed the interval in making inquiries, and I have at last discovered the hostile influence which has estranged you from me. I have been, it seems, so unfortunate as to offend Lady Lydiard (how, I cannot imagine); and the all-powerful influence of this noble lady is now used against the struggling artist who is united to you by the sacred ties of kindred. Be it so. I can fight my way upwards, my Lord, as other men have done before me. A day may yet come when the throng of carriages waiting at the door of the fashionable portrait-painter will include her Ladyship's vehicle, and bring me the tardy expression of her Ladyship's regret. I refer you, my Lord Lydiard, to that day!'

Having read Mr Tollmidge's formidable assertions relating to herself for the second time, Lady Lydiard's meditations came to an abrupt end. She rose, took the letters in both hands to tear them up, hesitated, and threw them back in the cabinet drawer in which she had discovered them, among other papers that had not been arranged since Lord Lydiard's death.

'The idiot!' said her Ladyship, thinking of Mr Tollmidge, 'I never even heard of him, in my husband's lifetime; I never even knew that he was really related to Lord Lydiard, till I found his letters. What is to be done next?'

She looked, as she put that question to herself, at an open newspaper thrown on the table, which announced the death of 'that accomplished artist Mr Tollmidge, related, it is said, to the late well-known connoisseur, Lord Lydiard.' In the next sentence the writer of the obituary notice deplored the destitute condition of Mrs Tollmidge and her children, 'thrown helpless on the mercy of the world.' Lady Lydiard stood by the table with her eyes on those lines, and saw but too plainly the direction in which they pointed – the direction of her cheque-book.

Turning towards the fireplace, she rang the bell. 'I can do nothing in this matter,' she thought to herself, 'until I know whether the report about Mrs Tollmidge and her family is to be depended on. Has Moody come back?' she asked, when the servant appeared at the door. 'Moody' (otherwise her Lady-ship's steward) had not come back. Lady Lydiard dismissed the subject of the artist's widow from further consideration until the steward returned, and gave her mind to a question of domestic interest which lay nearer to her heart. Her favourite dog had been ailing for some time past, and no report of him had reached her that morning. She opened a door near the fireplace, which led, through a little corridor hung with rare prints, to her own boudoir. 'Isabel!' she called out, 'how is Tommie?'

A fresh young voice answered from behind the curtain which closed the further end of the corridor, 'No better, my Lady.'

A low growl followed the fresh young voice, and added (in dog's language), 'Much worse, my Lady – much worse!'

Lady Lydiard closed the door again, with a compassionate sigh for Tommie, and walked slowly to and fro in her spacious drawing-room, waiting for the steward's return.

Accurately described, Lord Lydiard's widow was short and fat, and, in the matter of age, perilously near her sixtieth birthday. But it may be said, without paying a compliment, that she looked younger than her age by ten years at least. Her complexion was that of delicate pink tinge which is sometimes seen in old women with well-preserved constitutions. Her eyes (equally well preserved) were of that hard light blue colour which wears well, and does not wash out when tried by the test of tears. Add to this her short nose, her plump cheeks that set wrinkles at defiance, her white hair dressed in stiff little curls; and, if a doll could grow old, Lady Lydiard, at sixty, would have been the living image of that doll, taking life easily on its journey downwards to the prettiest of tombs, in a burial-ground where the myrtles and roses grew all the year round!

These being her Ladyship's personal merits, impartial his-tory must acknowledge, on the list of her defects, a total want of tact and taste in her attire. The lapse of time since Lord Lydiard's death had left her at liberty to dress as she pleased. She arrayed her short, clumsy figure in colours that were far too bright for a woman of her age. Her dresses, badly chosen as to their hues, were perhaps not badly made, but were certainly badly worn. Morally, as well as physically, it must be said of Lady Lydiard that her outward side was her worst side. The anomalies of her dress were matched by the anomalies of her character. There were moments when she felt and spoke as became a lady of rank; and there were other moments when she felt and spoke as might have become the cook in the kitchen. Beneath these superficial inconsistencies, the great heart, the essentially true and generous nature of the woman, only waited the sufficient occasion to assert themselves. In the trivial intercourse of society she was open to ridicule on every side of her. But when a serious emergency tried the metal of which she was really made, the people who were loudest in laughing at her stood aghast, and wondered what had become of the familiar companion of their everyday lives.

Her Ladyship's promenade had lasted but a little while, when a man in black clothing presented himself noiselessly at the great door which opened on the staircase. Lady Lydiard signed to him impatiently to enter the room.

'I have been expecting you for some time, Moody,' she said. 'You look tired. Take a chair.'

The man in black bowed respectfully, and took his seat.

CHAPTER II

Robert Moody was at this time nearly forty years of age. He was a shy, quiet, dark person, with a pale, closely-shaven face, agreeably animated by large black eyes, set deep in their orbits. His mouth was perhaps his best feature; he had firm, well-shaped lips, which softened on rare occasions into a particularly winning smile. The whole look of the man, in spite of his habitual reserve, declared him to be eminently trustworthy. His position in Lady Lydiard's household was in no sense of the menial sort. He acted as her almoner and secretary as well as her steward – distributed her charities, wrote her letters on business, paid her bills, engaged her servants, stocked her wine-cellar, was authorized to borrow books from her library, and was served with his meals in his own room. His parentage gave him claims to these special favours; he was by birth entitled to rank as a gentleman. His father had failed at a time of commercial panic as a country banker, had paid a good dividend, and had died in exile abroad a broken-hearted man. Robert had tried to hold his place in the world, but adverse fortune kept him down. Undeserved disaster followed him from one employment to another, until he abandoned the struggle, bade a last farewell to the pride of other days, and accepted the position considerately and delicately offered to him in Lady Lydiard's house. He had now no near relations living, and he had never made many friends. In the intervals of occupation he led a lonely life in his little room. It was a matter of secret wonder among the women in the servants' hall, considering his personal advantages and the opportunities which must surely have been thrown in his way, that he had never tempted fortune in the character of a married man. Robert Moody entered into no explanations on that subject. In his own sad and quiet way he continued to lead his own sad and quiet life. The women all failing, from the handsome housekeeper downwards, to make the smallest impression on him, consoled themselves by prophetic visions of his future relations with the sex, and predicted vindictively that 'his time would come.'

'Well,' said Lady Lydiard, 'and what have you done?'

'Your Ladyship seemed to be anxious about the dog,' Moody answered, in the low tone which was habitual to him. 'I went first to the veterinary surgeon. He had been called away into the country; and —— '

Lady Lydiard waved away the conclusion of the sentence with her hand. 'Never mind the surgeon. We must find somebody else. Where did you go next?'

'To your Ladyship's lawyer. Mr Troy wished me to say that he will have the honour of waiting on you —— '

'Pass over the lawyer, Moody. I want to know about the painter's widow. Is it true that Mrs Tollmidge and her family are left in helpless poverty?'

'Not quite true, my Lady. I have seen the clergyman of the parish, who takes an interest in the case —— '

Lady Lydiard interrupted her steward for the third time. 'Did you mention my name?' she asked sharply.

'Certainly not, my Lady. I followed my instructions, and described you as a benevolent person in search of cases of real distress. It is quite true that Mr Tollmidge has died, leaving nothing to his family. But the widow has a little income of seventy pounds in her own right.'

'Is that enough to live on, Moody?' her Ladyship asked.

'Enough, in this case, for the widow and her daughter,' Moody answered. 'The difficulty is to pay the few debts left standing, and to start the two sons in life. They are reported to be steady lads; and the family is much respected in the neighbourhood. The clergyman proposes to get a few influential names to begin with, and to start a subscription.'

'No subscription!' protested Lady Lydiard. 'Mr Tollmidge was Lord Lydiard's cousin; and Mrs Tollmidge is related to his Lordship by marriage. It would be degrading to my husband's memory to have the begging-box sent round for his relations, no matter how distant they may be. Cousins!' exclaimed her Ladyship, suddenly descending from the lofty ranges of sentiment to the low. 'I hate the very name of them! A person who is near enough to me to be my relation and far enough off from me to be my sweetheart, is a double-faced sort of person that I don't like. Let's get back to the widow and her sons. How much do they want?'

'A subscription of five hundred pounds, my Lady, would provide for everything – if it could only be collected.'

'It *shall* be collected, Moody! I will pay the subscription out of my own purse.' Having asserted herself in those noble terms, she spoilt the effect of her own outburst of generosity by dropping to the sordid view of the subject in her next sentence. 'Five hundred pounds is a good bit of money, though; isn't it, Moody?'

'It is, indeed, my Lady.' Rich and generous as he knew his mistress to be, her proposal to pay the whole subscription took the steward by surprise. Lady Lydiard's quick perception instantly detected what was passing in his mind.

'You don't quite understand my position in this matter,' she said. 'When I read the newspaper notice of Mr Tollmidge's death, I searched among his Lordship's papers to see if they really were related. I discovered some letters from Mr Toll-midge, which showed me that he and Lord Lydiard were cousins. One of those letters contains some very painful statements, reflecting most untruly and unjustly on my conduct; lies, in short,' her Ladyship burst out, losing her dignity, as usual. 'Lies, Moody, for which Mr Tollmidge deserved to be horsewhipped. I would have done it myself if his Lordship had told me at the time. No matter; it's useless to dwell on the thing now,' she continued, ascending again to the forms of expression which became a lady of rank. 'This unhappy man has done me a gross injustice; my motives may be seriously misjudged, if I appear personally in communicating with his family. If I relieve them anonymously in their present trouble, I spare them the exposure of a public subscription, and I do what I believe his Lordship would have done himself if he had lived. My desk is on the other table. Bring it here, Moody; and let me return good for evil, while I'm in the humour for it!'

Moody obeyed in silence. Lady Lydiard wrote a cheque.

'Take that to the banker's, and bring back a five-hundred pound note,' she said. 'I'll enclose it to the clergyman as coming from "an unknown friend". And be quick about it. I am only a fallible mortal, Moody. Don't leave me time enough to take the stingy view of five hundred pounds.'

Moody went out with the cheque. No delay was to be apprehended in obtaining the money; the banking-house was hard by, in St James's Street. Left alone, Lady Lydiard decided on occupying her mind in the generous direction by composing her anonymous letter to the clergyman. She had just taken a sheet of note-paper from her desk, when a servant appeared at the door announcing a visitor—

'Mr Felix Sweetsir!'

CHAPTER III

'My nephew!' Lady Lydiard exclaimed, in a tone which expressed astonishment, but certainly not pleasure as well.

'How many years is it since you and I last met?' she asked, in her abruptly straightforward way, as Mr Felix Sweetsir approached her writing-table.

The visitor was not a person easily discouraged. He took Lady Lydiard's hand, and kissed it with easy grace. A shade of irony was in his manner, agreeably relieved by a playful flash of tenderness.

'Years, my dear aunt?' he said. 'Look in your glass and you will see that time has stood still since we met last. How wonderfully well you wear! When shall we celebrate the appearance of your first wrinkle? I am too old; I shall never live to see it.'

He took an easy-chair, uninvited; placed himself close at his aunt's side, and ran his eye over her ill-chosen dress with an air of satirical admiration. 'How perfectly successful!' he said, with his well-bred insolence. 'What a chaste gaiety of colour!'

'What do you want?' asked her Ladyship, not in the least softened by the compliment.

'I want to pay my respects to my dear aunt,' Felix answered, perfectly impenetrable to his ungracious reception, and perfectly comfortable in a spacious arm-chair.

No pen-and-ink portrait need surely be drawn of Felix Sweetsir – he is too well-known a picture in society. The little lithe man, with his bright, restless eyes, and his long iron-grey hair falling in curls to his shoulders; his airy step and his cordial manner; his uncertain age, his innumerable accomplishments, and his unbounded popularity – is he not familiar everywhere, and welcome everywhere? How gratefully he receives, how prodigally he repays, the cordial appreciation of an admiring world! Every man he knows is 'a charming fellow'. Every woman he sees is 'sweetly pretty'. What picnics he gives on the banks of the Thames in the summer season! What a well-earned little income he derives from the whist-table! What an inestimable actor he is at private theatricals of all sorts (weddings included)! Did you never read Sweetsir's novel, dashed off in the intervals of curative perspiration at a German bath? Then you don't know what brilliant fiction really is. He has never written a second work; he does everything, and only does it once. One song – the despair of professional composers. One picture – just to show

how easily a gentleman can take up an art and drop it again. A really multiform man, with all the graces and all the accomplishments scintillating perpetually at his fingers' ends. If these poor pages have achieved nothing else, they have done a service to persons not in society by presenting them to Sweetsir. In his gracious company the narrative brightens; and writer and reader (catching reflected brilliancy) understand each other at last, thanks to Sweetsir.

'Well,' said Lady Lydiard, 'now you are here, what have you got to say for yourself? You have been abroad, of course! Where?'

'Principally at Paris, my dear aunt. The only place that is fit to live in – for this excellent reason, that the French are the only people who know how to make the most of life. One has relations and friends in England; and every now and then one returns to London —— '

'When one has spent all one's money in Paris,' her Ladyship interposed. 'That's what you were going to say, isn't it?'

Felix submitted to the interruption with his delightful good-humour.

'What a bright creature you are!' he exclaimed. 'What would I not give for your flow of spirits! Yes – one does spend money in Paris, as you say. The clubs, the stock exchange, the race-course: you try your luck here, there, and everywhere; and you lose and win, win and lose – and you haven't a dull day to complain of.' He paused, his smile died away, he looked inquiringly at Lady Lydiard. 'What a wonderful existence yours must be,' he resumed. 'The everlasting question with your needy fellow-creatures, "Where am I to get money?" is a question that has never passed your lips. Enviable woman!' He paused once more – surprised and puzzled this time. 'What is the matter, my dear aunt? You seem to be suffering under some uneasiness.'

'I am suffering under your conversation,' her Ladyship answered sharply. 'Money is a sore subject with me just now,' she went on, with her eyes on her nephew, watching the effect of what she said. 'I have spent five hundred pounds this morning with a scrape of my pen. And, only a week since, I yielded to temptation and made an addition to my picture-gallery.' She looked, as she said those words, towards an archway at the farther end of the room, closed by curtains of purple velvet. 'I really tremble when I think of what that one picture cost me before I could call it mine. A landscape by Hobbema; and the National Gallery bidding against me. Never mind!' she concluded, consoling herself, as usual, with considerations that were beneath her. 'Hobbema will sell at my death for a bigger price than I gave for him – that's one comfort!' She looked again at Felix; a smile of mischievous satisfaction began to show itself in her face. 'Anything wrong with your watch-chain?' she asked.

Felix, absently playing with his watch-chain, started as if his aunt had suddenly awakened him. While Lady Lydiard had been speaking, his vivacity had subsided little by little, and had left him looking so serious and so old that his most intimate friend would hardly have known him again. Roused by the sudden question that had been put to him, he seemed to be casting about in his mind in search of the first excuse for his silence that might turn up.

'I was wondering,' he began, 'why I miss something when I look round this beautiful room; something familiar, you know, that I fully expected to find here.'

'Tommie?' suggested Lady Lydiard, still watching her nephew as maliciously as ever.

'That's it!' cried Felix, seizing his excuse, and rallying his spirits. 'Why don't I hear Tommie snarling behind me; why don't I feel Tommie's teeth in my trousers?'

The smile vanished from Lady Lydiard's face; the tone taken by her nephew in speaking of her dog was disrespectful in the extreme. She showed him plainly that she disapproved of it. Felix went on, nevertheless, impenetrable to reproof of the silent sort. 'Dear little Tommie! So delightfully fat; and such an infernal temper! I don't know whether I hate him or love him. Where is he?'

'Ill in bed,' answered her ladyship, with a gravity which startled even Felix himself. 'I wish to speak to you about Tommie. You know everybody. Do you know of a good dog-doctor? The person I have employed so far doesn't at all satisfy me.'

'Professional person?' inquired Felix.

'Yes.'

'All humbugs, my dear aunt. The worse the dog gets the bigger the bill grows, don't you see? I have got the man for you – a gentleman. Knows more about horses and dogs than all the veterinary surgeons put together. We met in the boat yesterday crossing the Channel. You know him by name, of course? Lord Rotherfield's youngest son, Alfred Hardyman.'

'The owner of the stud farm? The man who has bred the famous race-horses?' cried Lady Lydiard. 'My dear Felix, how can I presume to trouble such a great personage about my dog?'

Felix burst into his genial laugh. 'Never was modesty more woefully out of place,' he rejoined. 'Hardyman is dying to be presented to your Ladyship. He has heard, like everybody, of the magnificent decorations of this house, and he is longing to see them. His chambers are close by, in Pall-Mall. If he is at home we will have him here in five minutes. Perhaps I had better see the dog first?'

Lady Lydiard shook her head. 'Isabel says he had better not be disturbed,' she answered. 'Isabel understands him better than anybody.'

Felix lifted his lively eyebrows with a mixed expression of curiosity and surprise. 'Who is Isabel?'

Lady Lydiard was vexed with herself for carelessly mentioning Isabel's name in her nephew's presence. Felix was not the sort of person whom she was desirous of admitting to her confidence in domestic matters. 'Isabel is an addition to my household since you were here last,' she answered shortly.

'Young and pretty?' inquired Felix. 'Ah! you look serious, and you don't answer me. Young and pretty, evidently. Which may I see first, the addition to your household or the addition to your picture-gallery? You look at the picture-gallery – I am answered again.' He rose to approach the archway, and stopped at his first step forward. 'A sweet girl is a dreadful responsibility, aunt,' he resumed, with an ironical assumption of gravity. 'Do you know, I shouldn't be surprised if Isabel, in the long run, cost you more than Hobbema. Who is this at the door?'

The person at the door was Robert Moody, returned from the bank. Mr Felix Sweetsir, being near-sighted, was obliged to fit his eye-glass in position before he could recognize the prime minister of Lady Lydiard's household.

'Ha! our worthy Moody. How well he wears! Not a grey hair on his head — and look at mine! What dye do you use, Moody? If he had my open disposition he would tell. As it is, he looks unutterable things, and holds his tongue. Ah! if I could only have held *my* tongue — when I was in the diplomatic service, you know — what a position I might have occupied by this time! Don't let me interrupt you, Moody, if you have anything to say to Lady Lydiard.'

Having acknowledged Mr Sweetsir's lively greeting by a formal bow, and a grave look of wonder which respectfully repelled that vivacious gentleman's flow of humour, Moody turned towards his mistress.

'Have you got the bank-note?' asked her Ladyship.

Moody laid the bank-note on the table.

'Am I in the way?' inquired Felix.

'No,' said his aunt. 'I have a letter to write; it won't occupy me for more than a few minutes. You can stay here, or go and look at the Hobbema, which you please.'

Felix made a second sauntering attempt to reach the picture-gallery. Arrived within a few steps of the entrance, he stopped again, attracted by an open cabinet of Italian workmanship, filled with rare old china. Being nothing if not a cultivated amateur, Mr Sweetsir paused to pay his passing tribute of admiration before the contents of the cabinet. 'Charming! charming!' he said to himself, with his head twisted appreciatively a little on one side. Lady Lydiard and Moody left him in undisturbed enjoyment of the china, and went on with the business of the bank-note.

'Ought we to take the number of the note, in case of accident?' asked her Ladyship.

Moody produced a slip of paper from his waistcoat pocket. 'I took the number, my Lady, at the bank.'

'Very well. You keep it. While I am writing my letter, suppose you direct the envelope. What is the clergyman's name?'

Moody mentioned the name and directed the envelope. Felix, happening to look round at Lady Lydiard and the steward while they were both engaged in writing, returned suddenly to the table as if he had been struck by a new idea.

'Is there a third pen?' he asked. 'Why shouldn't I write a line at once to Hardyman, aunt? The sooner you have his opinion about Tommie the better – don't you think so?'

Lady Lydiard pointed to the pen tray, with a smile. To show consideration for her dog was to seize irresistibly on the high-road to her favour. Felix set to work on his letter, in a large scrambling hand-writing, with plenty of ink and a noisy pen. 'I declare we are like clerks in an office,' he remarked, in his cheery way. 'All with our noses to the paper, writing as if we lived by it! Here, Moody, let one of the servants take this at once to Mr Hardyman's.'

The messenger was despatched. Robert returned, and waited near his mistress, with the directed envelope in his hand. Felix sauntered back slowly towards the picture-gallery, for the third time. In a moment more Lady Lydiard finished her letter, and folded up the bank-note in it. She had just taken the directed envelope from Moody, and had just placed the letter inside it, when a scream from the inner room, in which Isabel was nursing the sick dog, startled everybody. 'My Lady! my Lady!' cried the girl, distractedly, 'Tommie is in a fit? Tommie is dying!'

Lady Lydiard dropped the unclosed envelope on the table, and ran – yes, short as she was and fat as she was, ran – into the inner room. The two men, left together, looked at each other.

'Moody,' said Felix, in his lazily-cynical way, 'do you think if you or I were in a fit that her Ladyship would run? Bah! these are the things that shake one's faith in human nature. I feel infernally seedy. That cursed Channel passage – I tremble in my inmost stomach when I think of it. Get me something, Moody.'

'What shall I send you, sir?' Moody asked coldly.

'Some dry curaçoa and a biscuit. And let it be brought to me in the picture-gallery. Damn the dog! I'll go and look at Hobbema.'

This time he succeeded in reaching the archway, and disappeared behind the curtains of the picture-gallery.

CHAPTER IV

Left alone in the drawing-room, Moody looked at the unfastened envelope on the table.

Considering the value of the inclosure, might he feel justified in wetting the gum and securing the envelope for safety's sake? After thinking it over, Moody decided that he was not justified in meddling with the letter. On reflection, her Ladyship might have changes to make in it – or might have a postscript to add to what she had already written. Apart, too, from these considerations, was it reasonable to act as if Lady Lydiard's house was an hotel, perpetually open to the intrusion of strangers? Objects worth twice five hundred pounds in the aggregate were scattered about on the tables and in the unlocked cabinets all round him. Moody withdrew, without further hesitation, to order the light restorative prescribed for himself by Mr Sweetsir.

The footman who took the curaçoa into the picture-gallery found Felix recumbent on a sofa, admiring the famous Hobbema.

'Don't interrupt me,' he said peevishly, catching the servant in the act of staring at him. 'Put down the bottle and go!' Forbidden to look at Mr Sweetsir, the man's eyes as he left the gallery turned wonderingly towards the famous landscape. And what did he see? He saw one towering big cloud in the sky that threatened rain, two withered mahogany-coloured trees sorely in want of rain, a muddy road greatly the worse for rain, and a vagabond boy running home who was afraid of the rain. That was the picture, to the footman's eye. He took a gloomy view of the state of Mr Sweetsir's brains on his return to the servants' hall. 'A slate loose, poor devil!' That was the footman's report of the brilliant Felix.

Immediately on the servant's departure, the silence in the picture-gallery was broken by voices penetrating into it from the drawing-room. Felix rose to a sitting position on the sofa. He had recognized the voice of Alfred Hardyman saying, 'Don't disturb Lady Lydiard,' and the voice of Moody answering, 'I will just knock at the door of her Ladyship's room, sir; you will find Mr Sweetsir in the picture-gallery.'

The curtains over the archway parted, and disclosed the figure of a tall man, with a closely cropped head set a little stiffly on his shoulders. The immovable gravity of face and manner which every Englishman seems to acquire who lives constantly in the society of horses, was the gravity which this gentleman displayed as he entered the picture-gallery. He was a finely made, sinewy man, with clearly cut, regular features. If he had not been affected with horses on the brain he would doubtless have been personally popular with the women. As it was, the serene and hippic gloom of the handsome horse-breeder daunted the daughters of Eve, and they failed to make up their minds about the exact value of him, socially considered. Alfred Hardyman was nevertheless a remarkable man in his way. He had been offered the customary alternatives submitted to the younger sons of the nobility – the Church or the diplomatic service – and had refused the one and the other. 'I like horses,' he said, 'and I mean to get my living out of them. Don't talk to me about my position in the world. Talk to my eldest brother, who gets the money and the title.' Starting in life with these sensible views, and with a small capital of five thousand pounds, Hardyman took his own place in the sphere that was fitted for him. At the period of this narrative he was already a rich man, and one of the greatest authorities on horse-breeding in England. His prosperity made no change in him. He was always the same grave, quiet, obstinately resolute man – true to the few friends whom he admitted to his intimacy, and sincere to a fault in the expression of his feelings among persons whom he distrusted or disliked. As he entered the picture-gallery and paused for a moment looking at Felix on the sofa, his large, cold, steady grey eyes rested on the little man with an indifference that just verged on contempt. Felix, on the other hand, sprang to his feet with alert politeness and greeted his friend with exuberant cordiality.

'Dear old boy! This is so good of you,' he began. 'I feel it – I do assure you I feel it!'

'You needn't trouble yourself to feel it,' was the quietly-ungracious answer. 'Lady Lydiard brings me here. I come to see the house – and the dog.' He looked round the gallery in his gravely attentive way. 'I don't understand pictures,' he remarked resignedly. 'I shall go back to the drawing-room.'

After a moment's consideration, Felix followed him into the drawing-room, with the air of a man who was determined not to be repelled.

'Well?' asked Hardyman. 'What is it?'

'About that matter?' Felix said, inquiringly.

'What matter?'

'Oh, you know. Will next week do?'

'Next week *won't* do.'

Mr Felix Sweetsir cast one look at his friend. His friend was too intently occupied with the decorations of the drawing-room to notice the look.

'Will to-morrow do?' Felix resumed, after an interval.

'Yes.'

'At what time?'

'Between twelve and one in the afternoon.'

'Between twelve and one in the afternoon,' Felix repeated. He looked again at Hardyman and took his hat. 'Make my apologies to my aunt,' he said. 'You must introduce yourself to her Ladyship. I can't wait here any longer.' He walked out of the room, having deliberately returned the contemptuous indifference of Hardyman by a similar indifference on his own side, at parting.

Left by himself, Hardyman took a chair and glanced at the door which led into the boudoir. The steward had knocked at that door, had disappeared through it, and had not appeared again. How much longer was Lady Lydiard's visitor to be left unnoticed in Lady Lydiard's house?

As the question passed through his mind the boudoir door opened. For once in his life, Alfred Hardyman's composure deserted him. He started to his feet, like an ordinary mortal taken completely by suprise.

Instead of Mr Moody, instead of Lady Lydiard, there appeared in the open doorway a young woman in a state of embarrassment, who actually quickened the beat of Mr Hardyman's heart the moment he set eyes on her. Was the person who produced this amazing impression at first sight a person of importance? Nothing of the sort. She was only 'Isabel', surnamed 'Miller'. Even her name had nothing in it. Only 'Isabel Miller'!

Had she any pretensions to distinction in virtue of her personal appearance?

It is not easy to answer the question. The women (let us put the worst judges first) had long since discovered that she wanted that indispensable elegance of figure which is derived from slimness of waist and length of limb. The men (who were better acquainted with the subject) looked at her figure from their point of view; and, finding it essentially embraceable, asked for nothing more. It might have been her bright complexion, or it might have been the bold lustre of her eyes (as the women considered it), that dazzled the lords of creation generally, and made them all alike incompetent to discover her faults. Still, she had compensating attractions which no severity of criticism could dispute. Her smile, beginning at her lips, flowed brightly and instantly over her whole face. A delicious atmosphere of health, freshness, and good humour seemed to radiate from her wherever she went and whatever she did. For the rest, her brown hair grew low over her broad white forehead, and was topped by a neat little lace cap with ribbons of a violet colour. A plain collar and plain cuffs encircled her smooth, round neck, and her plump dimpled hands. Her merino dress, covering but not hiding the charming outline of her bosom, matched the colour of the cap-ribbons, and was brightened by a white muslin apron coquettishly trimmed about the pockets, a gift from Lady Lydiard. Blushing and smiling, she let the door fall to behind her, and, shyly approaching the stranger, said to him, in her small, clear voice, 'If you please, sir, are you Mr Hardyman?'

The gravity of the great horsebreeder deserted him at her first question. He smiled as he acknowledged that he was 'Mr Hardyman' – he smiled as he offered her a chair.

'No, thank you, sir,' she said, with a quaintly pretty inclination of her head. 'I am only sent here to make her Ladyship's apologies. She has put the poor dear dog into a warm bath, and she can't leave him. And Mr Moody can't come instead of me, because I was too frightened to be of any use, and so he had to hold the dog. That's all. We are very anxious, sir, to know if the warm bath is the right thing. Please come into the room and tell us.'

She led the way back to the door. Hardyman, naturally enough, was slow to follow her. When a man is fascinated by the charm of youth and beauty, he is in no hurry to transfer his attention to a sick animal in a bath. Hardyman seized on the first excuse that he could devise for keeping Isabel to himself – that is to say, for keeping her in the drawing-room.

'I think I shall be better able to help you,' he said, 'if you will tell me something about the dog first.'

Even his accent in speaking had altered to a certain degree. The quiet, dreary monotone in which he habitually spoke quickened a little under his present excitement. As for Isabel, she was too deeply interested in Tommie's welfare to suspect that she was being made the victim of a stratagem. She left the door and returned to Hardyman with eager eyes. 'What can I tell you, sir?' she asked innocently.

Hardyman pressed his advantage without mercy.

'You can tell me what sort of dog he is?'

'Yes, sir.'

'How old he is?'

'Yes, sir.'

'What his name is? – what his temper is? – what his illness is? what diseases his father and mother had? – what —— '

Isabel's head began to turn giddy. 'One thing at a time, sir!' she interposed, with a gesture of entreaty. 'The dog sleeps on my bed, and I had a bad night with him, he disturbed me so, and I am afraid I am very stupid this morning. His name is Tommie. We are obliged to call him by it, because he won't answer to any other than the name he had when my Lady bought him. But we spell it with an 'i e' at the end, which makes it less vulgar than Tommy with a 'y'. I am very sorry, sir – I forget what else you wanted to know. Please to come in here and my Lady will tell you everything.'

She tried to get back to the door of the boudoir. Hardyman, feasting his eyes on the pretty, changeful face that looked up at him with such innocent confidence in his authority, drew her away from the door by the one means at his disposal. He returned to his questions about Tommie.

'Wait a little, please. What sort of dog is he?'

Isabel turned back again from the door. To describe Tommie was a labour of love. 'He is the most beautiful dog in the world!' the girl began, with kindling eyes. 'He has the most exquisite white curly hair and two light brown patches on his back – and, oh! *such* lovely dark eyes! They call him a Scotch

terrier. When he is well his appetite is truly wonderful –
nothing comes amiss to him, sir, from pâté de foie gras to
potatoes. He has his enemies, poor dear, though you wouldn't
think it. People who won't put up with being bitten by him
(what shocking tempers one does meet with, to be sure!) call
him a mongrel. Isn't it a shame? Please come in and see him,
sir; my Lady will be tired of waiting.'

Another journey to the door followed those words, checked
instantly by a serious objection.

'Stop a minute! You must tell me what his temper is, or I
can do nothing for him.'

Isabel returned once more, feeling that it was really serious
this time. Her gravity was even more charming than her
gaiety. As she lifted her face to him, with large solemn eyes,
expressive of her sense of responsibility, Hardyman would
have given every horse in his stables to have had the privilege
of taking her in his arms and kissing her.

'Tommie has the temper of an angel with the people he
likes,' she said. 'When he bites, it generally means that he
objects to strangers. He loves my Lady, and he loves Mr
Moody, and he loves me, and – and I think that's all. This
way, sir, if you please, I am sure I heard my Lady call.'

'No,' said Hardyman, in his immovably obstinate way.
'Nobody called. About this dog's temper? Doesn't he take to
any strangers? What sort of people does he bite in general?'

Isabel's pretty lips began to curl upward at the corners in a
quaint smile. Hardyman's last imbecile question had opened
her eyes to the true state of the case. Still, Tommie's future
was in this strange gentleman's hands; she felt bound to
consider that. And, moreover, it was no everyday event, in
Isabel's experience, to fascinate a famous personage, who was
also a magnificent and perfectly dressed man. She ran the risk
of wasting another minute or two, and went on with the
memoirs of Tommie.

'I must own, sir,' she resumed, 'that he behaves a little
ungratefully – even to strangers who take an interest in him.
When he gets lost in the streets (which is very often), he sits
down on the pavement and howls till he collects a pitying
crowd round him; and when they try to read his name and
address on his collar he snaps at them. The servants generally

find him and bring him back; and as soon as he gets home he turns round on the doorstep and snaps at the servants. I think it must be his fun. You should see him sitting up in his chair at dinner-time, waiting to be helped, with his fore paws on the edge of the table, like the hands of a gentleman at a public dinner making a speech. But, oh!' cried Isabel, checking herself, with the tears in her eyes, 'how can I talk of him in this way when he is so dreadfully ill! Some of them say it's bronchitis, and some say it's his liver. Only yesterday I took him to the front door to give him a little air, and he stood still on the pavement, quite stupefied. For the first time in his life, he snapped at nobody who went by; and, oh, dear, he hadn't even the heart to smell a lamp-post!'

Isabel had barely stated this last afflicting circumstance when the memoirs of Tommie were suddenly cut short by the voice of Lady Lydiard – really calling this time – from the inner room.

'Isabel! Isabel!' cried her Ladyship, 'what are you about?'

Isabel ran to the door of the boudoir and threw it open. 'Go in, sir! Pray go in!' she said.

'Without you?' Hardyman asked.

'I will follow you, sir. I have something to do for her Ladyship first.'

She still held the door open, and pointed entreatingly to the passage which led to the boudoir. 'I shall be blamed, sir,' she said, 'if you don't go in.'

This statement of the case left Hardyman no alternative. He presented himself to Lady Lydiard without another moment of delay.

Having closed the drawing-room door on him, Isabel waited a little, absorbed in her own thoughts.

She was now perfectly well aware of the effect which she had produced on Hardyman. Her vanity, it is not to be denied, was flattered by his admiration – he was so grand and so tall, and he had such fine large eyes. The girl looked prettier than ever as she stood with her head down and her colour heightened, smiling to herself. A clock on the chimneypiece striking the half-hour roused her. She cast one look at the glass, as she passed it, and went to the table at which Lady Lydiard had been writing.

Methodical Mr Moody, in submitting to be employed as bath-attendant upon Tommie, had not forgotten the interests of his mistress. He reminded her Ladyship that she had left her letter, with a bank-note inclosed in it, unsealed. Absorbed in the dog, Lady Lydiard answered, 'Isabel is doing nothing, let Isabel seal it. Show Mr Hardyman in here,' she continued, turning to Isabel, 'and then seal a letter of mine which you will find on the table.' 'And when you have sealed it,' careful Mr Moody added, 'put it back on the table; I will take charge of it when her Ladyship has done with me.'

Such were the special instructions which now detained Isabel in the drawing-room. She lit the taper, and closed and sealed the open envelope, without feeling curiosity enough even to look at the address. Mr Hardyman was the uppermost subject in her thoughts. Leaving the sealed letter on the table, she returned to the fireplace, and studied her own charming face attentively in the looking-glass. The time passed – and Isabel's reflection was still the subject of Isabel's contemplation. 'He must see many beautiful ladies,' she thought, veering backwards and forwards between pride and humility. 'I wonder what he sees in Me?'

The clock struck the hour. Almost at the same moment the boudoir-door opened, and Robert Moody, released at last from attendance on Tommie, entered the drawing-room.

CHAPTER V

'Well?' asked Isabel eagerly, 'what does Mr Hardyman say? Does he think he can cure Tommie?'

Moody answered a little coldly and stiffly. His dark, deeply set eyes rested on Isabel with an uneasy look.

'Mr Hardyman seems to understand animals,' he said. 'He lifted the dog's eyelid and looked at his eyes, and then he told us the bath was useless.'

'Go on!' said Isabel impatiently. 'He did something, I suppose, besides telling you that the bath was useless?'

'He took a knife out of his pocket, with a lancet in it.'

Isabel clasped her hands with a faint cry of horror. 'Oh, Mr Moody! did he hurt Tommie?'

'Hurt him?' Moody repeated, indignant at the interest which she felt in the animal, and the indifference which she exhibited towards the man (as represented by himself). 'Hurt him, indeed! Mr Hardyman bled the brute – '

'Brute?' Isabel reiterated, with flashing eyes. 'I know some people, Mr Moody, who really deserve to be called by that horrid word. If you can't say "Tommie" when you speak of him in my presence, be so good as to say "the dog".'

Moody yielded with the worst possible grace. 'Oh, very well! Mr Hardyman bled the dog, and brought him to his senses directly. I am charged to tell you —— ' He stopped, as if the message which he was instructed to deliver was in the last degree distasteful to him.

'Well, what were you charged to tell me?'

'I was to say that Mr Hardyman will give you instructions how to treat the dog for the future.'

Isabel hastened to the door, eager to receive her instructions. Moody stopped her before she could open it.

'You are in a great hurry to get to Mr Hardyman,' he remarked.

Isabel looked back at him in surprise. 'You said just now that Mr Hardyman was waiting to tell me how to nurse Tommie.'

'Let him wait,' Moody rejoined sternly. 'When I left him, he was sufficiently occupied in expressing his favourable opinion of you to her Ladyship.'

The steward's pale face turned paler still as he said those words. With the arrival of Isabel in Lady Lydiard's house 'his time had come' – exactly as the women in the servants' hall had predicted. At last the impenetrable man felt the influence of the sex; at last he knew the passion of love – misplaced, ill-starred, hopeless love, for a woman who was young enough to be his child. He had already spoken to Isabel more than once in terms which told his secret plainly enough. But the smouldering fire of jealousy in the man, fanned into flame by Hardyman, now showed itself for the first time. His looks, even more than his words, would have warned a woman with any knowledge of the natures of men to be careful how she answered him. Young, giddy, and inexperienced, Isabel followed the flippant impulse of the moment, without a thought of the consequences. 'I'm sure it's very kind of Mr Hardyman to speak favourably of me,' she said, with a pert little laugh. 'I hope you are not jealous of him, Mr Moody?'

Moody was in no humour to make allowances for the unbridled gaiety of youth and good spirits. 'I hate any man who admires you,' he burst out passionately, 'let him be who he may!'

Isabel looked at her strange lover with unaffected astonishment. How unlike Mr Hardyman, who had treated her as a lady from first to last! 'What an odd man you are!' she said. 'You can't take a joke. I'm sure I didn't mean to offend you.'

'You don't offend me – you do worse, you distress me.'

Isabel's colour began to rise. The merriment died out of her face; she looked at Moody gravely. 'I don't like to be accused of distressing people when I don't deserve it,' she said. 'I had better leave you. Let me by, if you please.'

Having committed one error in offending her, Moody committed another in attempting to make his peace with her. Acting under the fear that she would really leave him, he took her roughly by the arm.

'You are always trying to get away from me,' he said. 'I wish I knew how to make you like me, Isabel.'

'I don't allow you to call me Isabel!' she retorted, struggling to free herself from his hold. 'Let go of my arm. You hurt me.'

Moody dropped her arm with a bitter sigh. 'I don't know how to deal with you,' he said simply. 'Have some pity on me!'

If the steward had known anything of women (at Isabel's age) he would never have appealed to her mercy in those plain terms, and at the unpropitious moment. 'Pity you?' she repeated contemptuously. 'Is that all you have to say to me after hurting my arm? What a bear you are!' She shrugged her shoulders and put her hands coquettishly into the pockets of her apron. That was how she pitied him! His face turned paler and paler – he writhed under it.

'For God's sake, don't turn everything I say to you into ridicule!' he cried. 'You know I love you with all my heart and soul. Again and again I have asked you to be my wife – and you laugh at me as if it was a joke. I haven't deserved to be treated in that cruel way. It maddens me – I can't endure it!'

Isabel looked down on the floor, and followed the lines in the pattern of the carpet with the end of her smart little shoe. She could hardly have been farther away from really understanding Moody if he had spoken in Hebrew. She was partly startled, partly puzzled, by the strong emotions which she had unconsciously called into being. 'Oh dear me!' she said, 'why can't you talk of something else? Why can't we be friends? Excuse me for mentioning it,' she went on, looking up at him with a saucy smile, 'you are old enough to be my father.'

Moody's head sank on his breast. 'I own it,' he answered humbly. 'But there is something to be said for me. Men as old as I am have made good husbands before now. I would devote my whole life to make you happy. There isn't a wish you could form which I wouldn't be proud to obey. You musn't reckon me by years. My youth has not been wasted in a profligate life; I can be truer to you and fonder of you than many a younger man. Surely my heart is not quite unworthy of you, when it is all yours. I have lived such a lonely, miserable life – and you might so easily brighten it. You are kind to everybody else, Isabel. Tell me, dear, why are you so hard on *me*?'

His voice trembled as he appealed to her in those simple words. He had taken the right way at last to produce an impression on her. She really felt for him. All that was true and tender in her nature began to rise in her and take his part. Unhappily, he felt too deeply and too strongly to be patient, and give her time. He completely misinterpreted her silence – completely mistook the motive that made her turn aside for a moment, to gather composure enough to speak to him. 'Ah!' he burst out bitterly, turning away on his side, 'you have no heart.'

She instantly resented those unjust words. At that moment they wounded her to the quick.

'You know best,' she said. 'I have no doubt you are right. Remember one thing, however, though I have no heart, I have never encouraged you, Mr Moody. I have declared over and over again that I could only be your friend. Understand that for the future, if you please. There are plenty of nice women who will be glad to marry you, I have no doubt. You will always have my best wishes for your welfare. Good morning. Her Ladyship will wonder what has become of me. Be so kind as to let me pass.'

Tortured by the passion that consumed him, Moody obstinately kept his place between Isabel and the door. The unworthy suspicion of her, which had been in his mind all through the interview, now forced its way outwards to expression at last.

'No woman ever used a man as you use me without some reason for it,' he said. 'You have kept your secret wonderfully well – but sooner or later all secrets get found out. I know what is in your mind as well as you know it yourself. You are in love with some other man.'

Isabel's face flushed deeply; the defensive pride of her sex was up in arms in an instant. She cast one disdainful look at Moody, without troubling herself to express her contempt in words. 'Stand out of my way, sir!' – that was all she said to him.

'You are in love with some other man,' he reiterated passionately. 'Deny it if you can!'

'Deny it?' she repeated with flashing eyes. 'What right have you to ask the question? Am I not free to do as I please?'

He stood looking at her, meditating his next words with a sudden and sinister change to self-restraint. Suppressed rage was in his rigidly set eyes, suppressed rage was in his trembling hand as he raised it emphatically while he spoke his next words.

'I have one thing more to say,' he answered, 'and then I have done. If I am not your husband, no other man shall be. Look well to it, Isabel Miller. If there *is* another man between us, I can tell him this – he shall find it no easy matter to rob me of you!'

She started, and turned pale – but it was only for a moment. The high spirit that was in her rose brightly in her eyes, and faced him without shrinking.

'Threats?' she said with quiet contempt. 'When you make love, Mr Moody, you take strange ways of doing it. My

conscience is easy. You may try to frighten me, but you will
not succeed. When you have recovered your temper I will
accept your excuses.' She paused, and pointed to the table.
'There is the letter that you told me to leave for you when I
had sealed it,' she went on. 'I suppose you have her Ladyship's
orders. Isn't it time you began to think of obeying them?'

The contemptuous composure of her tone and manner
seemed to act on Moody with crushing effect. Without a word
of answer, the unfortunate steward took up the letter from the
table. Without a word of answer, he walked mechanically to
the great door which opened on the staircase – turned on the
threshold to look at Isabel – waited a moment, pale and still –
and suddenly left the room.

That silent departure, that hopeless submission, impressed
Isabel in spite of herself. The sustaining sense of injury and
insult sank, as it were, from under her the moment she was
alone. He had not been gone a minute before she began to be
sorry for him once more. The interview had taught her
nothing. She was neither old enough nor experienced enough
to understand the overwhelming revolution produced in a
man's character when he feels the passion of love for the first
time in the maturity of his life. If Moody had stolen a kiss at
the first opportunity, she would have resented the liberty he
had taken with her; but she would have thoroughly understood him. His terrible earnestness, his overpowering
agitation, his abrupt violence – all these evidences of a passion
that was a mystery to himself – simply puzzled her. 'I'm sure I
didn't wish to hurt his feelings' (such was the form that her
reflections took, in her present penitent frame of mind); 'but
why did he provoke me? It is a shame to tell me that I love
some other man – when there is no other man. I declare I
begin to hate the men, if they are all like Mr Moody. I wonder
whether he will forgive me when he sees me again? I'm sure
I'm willing to forget and forgive on my side – especially if he
won't insist on my being fond of him because he is fond of
me. Oh, dear! I wish he would come back and shake hands.
It's enough to try the patience of a saint to be treated in this
way. I wish I was ugly! The ugly ones have a quiet time of it –
the men let them be. Mr Moody! Mr Moody!' She went out to
the landing and called to him softly. There was no answer. He

was no longer in the house. She stood still for a moment in silent vexation. 'I'll go to Tommie!' she decided. 'I'm sure he's the more agreeable company of the two. And – oh, good gracious! there's Mr Hardyman waiting to give me my instructions! How do I look, I wonder?'

She consulted the glass once more – gave one or two corrective touches to her hair and her cap – and hastened into the boudoir.

CHAPTER VI

For a quarter of an hour the drawing-room remained empty. At the end of that time the council in the boudoir broke up. Lady Lydiard led the way back into the drawing-room, followed by Hardyman, Isabel being left to look after the dog. Before the door closed behind him, Hardyman turned round to reiterate his last medical directions – or, in plainer words, to take a last look at Isabel.

'Plenty of water, Miss Isabel, for the dog to lap, and a little bread or biscuit, if he wants something to eat. Nothing more, if you please, till I see him to-morrow.'

'Thank you, sir. I will take the greatest care —— '

At that point Lady Lydiard cut short the interchange of instructions and civilities. 'Shut the door, if you please, Mr Hardyman. I feel the draught. Many thanks! I am really at a loss to tell you how gratefully I feel your kindness. But for you my poor little dog might be dead by this time.'

Hardyman answered, in the quiet melancholy monotone which was habitual with him, 'Your Ladyship need feel no further anxiety about the dog. Only be careful not to overfeed him. He will do very well under Miss Isabel's care. By the bye, her family name is Miller – is it not? Is she related to the Warwickshire Millers of Duxborough House?'

Lady Lydiard looked at him with an expression of satirical surprise. 'Mr Hardyman,' she said, 'this makes the fourth time you have questioned me about Isabel. You seem to take a great interest in my little companion. Don't make any apologies, pray! You pay Isabel a compliment; and, as I am very fond of her, I am naturally gratified when I find her admired. At the same time,' she added, with one of her abrupt transitions of language, 'I had my eye on you, and I had my eye on her, when you were talking in the next room; and I don't mean to let you make a fool of the girl. She is not in your line of life, and the sooner you know it the better. You make me laugh when you ask if she is related to gentlefolks. She is the orphan daughter of a chemist in the country. Her relations haven't a penny to bless themselves with; except an old aunt, who lives in a village on two or three hundred a year. I heard of the girl by accident. When she lost her father and mother, her aunt offered to take her. Isabel said, "No, thank you; I will not be a burden on a relation who has only enough for herself. A girl can earn an honest living if she tries; and I mean to try" – that's what she said. I admired her independence,' her Ladyship proceeded, ascending again to the higher regions of thought and expression. 'My niece's marriage, just at that time, had left me alone in this great house. I proposed to Isabel to come to me as companion and reader for a few weeks, and to decide for herself whether she liked the life or not. We have never been separated since that time. I could hardly be fonder of her if she were my own daughter; and she returns my affection with all her heart. She has excellent qualities – prudent, cheerful, sweet-tempered; with good sense enough to understand what her place is in the world, as distinguished from her place in my regard. I have taken care, for her own sake, never to leave that part of the question in any doubt. It would be cruel kindness to deceive her as to her future position when she marries. I shall take good care that the man who pays his addresses to her is a man in her rank of life. I know but too well, in the case of one of my own relatives, what miseries unequal marriages bring with them. Excuse me for troubling you at this length on domestic matters. I am very fond of Isabel; and a girl's head is so easily turned. Now you know what her position really is, you will also know what limits there must be to the expression of your interest in her. I am sure we understand each other; and I say no more.'

Hardyman listened to this long harangue with the immovable gravity which was part of his character – except when

Isabel had taken him by surprise. When her Ladyship gave him the opportunity of speaking on his side, he had very little to say, and that little did not suggest that he had greatly profited by what he had heard. His mind had been full of Isabel when Lady Lydiard began, and it remained just as full of her, in just the same way, when Lady Lydiard had done.

'Yes,' he remarked quietly, 'Miss Isabel is an uncommonly nice girl, as you say. Very pretty, and such frank, unaffected manners. I don't deny that I feel an interest in her. The young ladies one meets in society are not much to my taste. Miss Isabel is my taste.'

Lady Lydiard's face assumed a look of blank dismay. 'I am afraid I have failed to convey my exact meaning to you,' she said.

Hardyman gravely declared that he understood her perfectly. 'Perfectly!' he repeated, with his impenetrable obstinacy. 'Your Ladyship exactly expresses my opinion of Miss Isabel. Prudent, and cheerful, and sweet-tempered, as you say – all the qualities in a woman that I admire. With good looks, too – of course, with good looks. She will be a perfect treasure (as you remarked just now) to the man who marries her. I may claim to know something about it. I have twice narrowly escaped being married myself; and, though I can't exactly explain it, I'm all the harder to please in consequence. Miss Isabel pleases me. I think I have said that before? Pardon me for saying it again. I'll call again to-morrow morning and look at the dog, as early as eleven o'clock, if you will allow me. Later in the day I must be off to France to attend a sale of horses. Glad to have been of any use to your Ladyship, I am sure. Good morning.'

Lady Lydiard let him go, wisely resigning any further attempt to establish an understanding between her visitor and herself.

'He is either a person of very limited intelligence when he is away from his stables,' she thought, 'or he deliberately declines to take a plain hint when it is given to him. I can't drop his acquaintance, on Tommie's account. The only other alternative is to keep Isabel out of his way. My good little girl shall not drift into a false position while I am living to look after her. When Mr Hardyman calls to-morrow she shall be

out on an errand. When he calls the next time she shall be
upstairs with a headache. And if he tries it again she shall be
away at my house in the country. If he makes any remarks on
her absence – well, he will find that I can be just as dull of
understanding as he is when the occasion calls for it.'

Having arrived at this satisfactory solution of the difficulty,
Lady Lydiard became conscious of an irresistible impulse to
summon Isabel to her presence and caress her. In the nature of
a warm-hearted woman, this was only the inevitable reaction
which followed the subsidence of anxiety about the girl, after
her own resolution had set that anxiety at rest. She threw open
the door and made one of her sudden appearances at the
boudoir. Even in the fervent outpouring of her affection, there
was still the inherent abruptness of manner which so strongly
marked Lady Lydiard's character in all the relations of life.

'Did I give you a kiss, this morning?' she asked, when Isabel
rose to receive her.

'Yes, my Lady,' said the girl, with her charming smile.

'Come, then, and give me a kiss in return. Do you love me?
Very well, then, treat me like your mother. Never mind "my
Lady" this time. Give me a good hug!'

Something in those homely words, or something perhaps in
the look that accompanied them, touched sympathies in Isabel
which seldom showed themselves on the surface. Her smiling
lips trembled, the bright tears rose in her eyes. 'You are too
good to me,' she murmured, with her head on Lady Lydiard's
bosom. 'How can I ever love you enough in return?'

Lady Lydiard patted the pretty head that rested on her with
such filial tenderness. 'There! there!' she said, 'Go back and
play with Tommie, my dear. We may be as fond of each other
as we like; but we mustn't cry. God bless you! Go away – go
away!'

She turned aside quickly; her own eyes were moistening,
and it was part of her character to be reluctant to let Isabel see
it. 'Why have I made a fool of myself?' she wondered, as she
approached the drawing-room door. 'It doesn't matter. I am
all the better for it. Odd, that Mr Hardyman should have
made me feel fonder of Isabel than ever!'

With those reflections she re-entered the drawing-room –
and suddenly checked herself with a start. 'Good Heavens!'

she exclaimed irritably, 'how you frightened me! Why was I not told you were here?'

Having left the drawing-room in a state of solitude, Lady Lydiard on her return found herself suddenly confronted with a gentleman, mysteriously planted on the hearth-rug in her absence. The new visitor may be rightly described as a grey man. He had grey hair, eyebrows, and whiskers; he wore a grey coat, waistcoat, and trousers, and grey gloves. For the rest, his appearance was eminently suggestive of wealth and respectability – and, in this case, appearances were really to be trusted. The grey man was no other than Lady Lydiard's legal adviser, Mr Troy.

'I regret, my Lady, that I should have been so unfortunate as to startle you,' he said, with a certain underlying embarrassment in his manner. 'I had the honour of sending word by Mr Moody that I would call at this hour, on some matters of business connected with your Ladyship's house property. I presumed that you expected to find me here, waiting your pleasure ——'

Thus far Lady Lydiard had listened to her legal adviser, fixing her eyes on his face in her usually frank, straightforward way. She now stopped him in the middle of a sentence, with a change of expression in her own face which was undisguisedly a change to alarm.

'Don't apologise, Mr Troy,' she said. 'I am to blame for forgetting your appointment, and for not keeping my nerves under proper control.' She paused for a moment, and took a seat before she said her next words. 'May I ask,' she resumed, 'if there is something unpleasant in the business that brings you here?'

'Nothing whatever, my Lady; mere formalities, which can wait till to-morrow or next day, if you wish it.'

Lady Lydiard's fingers drummed impatiently on the table. 'You have known me long enough, Mr Troy, to know that I cannot endure suspense. You *have* something unpleasant to tell me.'

The lawyer respectfully remonstrated. 'Really, Lady Lydiard! —— ' he began.

'It won't do, Mr Troy! I know how you look at me on ordinary occasions, and I see how you look at me now. You are a very clever lawyer; but, happily for the interests that I commit to your charge, you are also a thoroughly honest man. After twenty years' experience of you, you can't deceive *me*. You bring me bad news. Speak at once, sir, and speak plainly.'

Mr Troy yielded – inch by inch, as it were. 'I bring news which, I fear, may annoy your Ladyship.' He paused, and advanced another inch. 'It is news which I only became acquainted with myself on entering this house.' He waited again, and made another advance. 'I happened to meet your Ladyship's steward, Mr Moody, in the hall —— '

'Where is he?' Lady Lydiard interposed angrily. 'I can make *him* speak out, and I will. Send him here instantly.'

The lawyer made a last effort to hold off the coming disclosure a little longer. 'Mr Moody will be here directly,' he said. 'Mr Moody requested me to prepare your Lady-ship ——'

'Will you ring the bell, Mr Troy, or must I?'

Moody had evidently been waiting outside while the lawyer spoke for him. He saved Mr Troy the trouble of ringing the bell by presenting himself in the drawing-room. Lady Lydiard's eyes searched his face as he approached. Her bright complexion faded suddenly. Not a word more passed her lips. She looked, and waited.

In silence on his part, Moody laid an open sheet of paper on the table. The paper quivered in his trembling hand.

Lady Lydiard recovered herself first. 'Is that for me?' she asked.

'Yes, my Lady.'

She took up the paper without an instant's hesitation. Both the men watched her anxiously as she read it.

The handwriting was strange to her. The words were these:

'I hearby certify that the bearer of these lines, Robert Moody by name, has presented to me the letter with which he was charged, addressed to myself, with the seal intact. I regret to add that there is, to say the least of it, some mistake. The inclosure referred to by the anonymous writer of the letter, who signs "a friend in need", has not reached me. No five hundred pound bank-note was in the letter when I opened it. My wife was present when I broke the seal, and can certify to this statement if necessary. Not knowing who my charitable correspondent is (Mr Moody being forbidden to give me any information), I can only take this means of stating the case exactly as it stands, and hold myself at the disposal of the writer of the letter. My private address is at the head of the page. – Samuel Bradstock, Rector, St Anne's, Deansbury, London.'

Lady Lydiard dropped the paper on the table. For the moment, plainly as the Rector's statement was expressed, she appeared to be incapable of understanding it. 'What, in God's name, does this mean?' she asked.

The lawyer and the steward looked at each other. Which of the two was entitled to speak first? Lady Lydiard gave them no time to decide. 'Moody,' she said sternly, 'you took charge of the letter – I look to you for an explanation.'

Moody's dark eyes flashed. He answered Lady Lydiard without caring to conceal that he resented the tone in which she had spoken to him.

'I undertook to deliver the letter at its address,' he said. 'I found it, sealed, on the table. Your Ladyship has the clergyman's written testimony that I handed it to him with the seal unbroken. I have done my duty; and I have no explanation to offer.'

Before Lady Lydiard could speak again, Mr Troy discreetly interfered. He saw plainly that his experience was required to lead the investigation in the right direction.

'Pardon me, my Lady,' he said, with that happy mixture of the positive and the polite in his manner, of which lawyers alone possess the secret. 'There is only one way of arriving at the truth in painful matters of this sort. We must begin at the beginning. May I venture to ask your Ladyship a question?'

Lady Lydiard felt the composing influence of Mr Troy. 'I am at your disposal, sir,' she said quietly.

'Are you absolutely certain that you enclosed the bank-note in the letter?' the lawyer asked.

'I certainly believe I enclosed it,' Lady Lydiard answered. 'But I was so alarmed at the time by the sudden illness of my dog, that I do not feel justified in speaking positively.'

'Was anybody in the room with your Ladyship when you put the inclosure in the letter – as you believe?'

'*I* was in the room,' said Moody. 'I can swear that I saw her

Ladyship put the bank-note in the letter, and the letter in the envelope.'

'And seal the envelope?' asked Mr Troy.

'No, sir. Her Ladyship was called away into the next room to the dog, before she could seal the envelope.'

Mr Troy addressed himself once more to Lady Lydiard. 'Did your Ladyship take the letter into the next room with you?'

'I was too much alarmed to think of it, Mr Troy. I left it here, on the table.'

'With the envelope open?'

'Yes.'

'How long were you absent in the other room?'

'Half an hour or more.'

'Ha!' said Mr Troy to himself. 'This complicates it a little.' He reflected for a while, and then turned again to Moody. 'Did any of the servants know of this bank-note being in her Ladyship's possession?'

'Not one of them,' Moody answered.

'Do you suspect any of the servants?'

'Certainly not, sir.'

'Are there any workmen employed in the house?'

'No, sir.'

'Do you know of any persons who had access to the room while Lady Lydiard was absent from it?'

'Two visitors called, sir.'

'Who were they?'

'Her Ladyship's nephew, Mr Felix Sweetsir, and the Honourable Alfred Hardyman.'

Mr Troy shook his head irritably. 'I am not speaking of gentlemen of high position and repute,' he said. 'It's absurd even to mention Mr Sweetsir and Mr Hardyman. My question related to strangers who might have obtained access to the drawing-room – people calling, with her Ladyship's sanction, for subscriptions, for instance; or people calling with articles of dress or ornament to be submitted to her Ladyship's inspection.'

'No such persons came to the house with my knowledge,' Moody answered.

Mr Troy suspended the investigation, and took a turn thoughtfully in the room. The theory on which his inquiries had proceeded thus far had failed to produce any results. His experience warned him to waste no more time on it, and to return to the starting-point of the investigation – in other words, to the letter. Shifting his point of view, he turned again to Lady Lydiard, and tried his questions in a new direction.

'Mr Moody mentioned just now,' he said, 'that your Ladyship was called into the next room before you could seal your letter. On your return to this room, did you seal the letter?'

'I was busy with the dog,' Lady Lydiard answered. 'Isabel Miller was of no use in the boudoir, and I told her to seal it for me.'

Mr Troy started. The new direction in which he was pushing his inquiries began to look like the right direction already. 'Miss Isabel Miller,' he proceeded, 'has been a resident under your Ladyship's roof for some little time, I believe?'

'For nearly two years, Mr Troy.'

'As your Ladyship's companion and reader?'

'As my adopted daughter,' her Ladyship answered, with marked emphasis.

Wise Mr Troy rightly interpreted the emphasis as a warning to him to suspend the examination of her Ladyship, and to address to Mr Moody the far more serious questions which were now to come.

'Did anyone give you the letter before you left the house with it?' he said to the steward. 'Or did you take it yourself?'

'I took it myself, from the table here.'

'Was it sealed?'

'Yes.'

'Was anybody present when you took the letter from the table?'

'Miss Isabel was present.'

'Did you find her alone in the room?'

'Yes, sir.'

Lady Lydiard opened her lips to speak, and checked herself. Mr Troy, having cleared the ground before him, put the fatal question.

'Mr Moody,' he said, 'when Miss Isabel was instructed to seal the letter, did she know that a bank-note was inclosed in it?'

Instead of replying, Robert drew back from the lawyer with a look of horror. Lady Lydiard started to her feet – and checked herself again, on the point of speaking.

'Answer him, Moody,' she said, putting a strong constraint on herself.

Robert answered very unwillingly. 'I took the liberty of reminding her ladyship that she had left her letter unsealed,' he said. 'And I mentioned as my excuse for speaking' – he stopped, and corrected himself – 'I *believe* I mentioned that a valuable inclosure was in the letter.'

'You believe?' Mr Troy repeated. 'Can't you speak more positively than that?'

'*I* can speak positively,' said Lady Lydiard, with her eyes on the lawyer. 'Moody did mention the inclosure in the letter – in Isabel Miller's hearing as well as in mine.' She paused, steadily controlling herself. 'And what of that, Mr Troy?' she added, very quietly and firmly.

Mr Troy answered quietly and firmly, on his side. 'I am surprised that your Ladyship should ask the question,' he said.

'I persist in repeating the question,' Lady Lydiard rejoined. 'I say that Isabel Miller knew of the inclosure in my letter – and I ask, What of that?'

'And I answer,' retorted the impenetrable lawyer, 'that the suspicion of theft rests on your Ladyship's adopted daughter, and on nobody else.'

'It's false!' cried Robert, with a burst of honest indignation. 'I wish to God I had never said a word to you about the loss of the bank-note! Oh, my Lady! my Lady! don't let him distress you! What does *he* know about it?'

'Hush!' said Lady Lydiard. 'Control yourself, and hear what he has to say.' She rested her hand on Moody's shoulder, partly to encourage him, partly to support herself; and, fixing her eyes again on Mr Troy, repeated his last words, '"Suspicion rests on my adopted daughter, and on nobody else." Why on nobody else?'

'Is your Ladyship prepared to suspect the Rector of St Anne's of embezzlement, or your own relatives and equals of theft?' Mr Troy asked. 'Does a shadow of doubt rest on the servants? Not if Mr Moody's evidence is to be believed. Who, to our own certain knowledge, had access to the letter while it was unsealed? Who was alone in the room with it? And who knew of the inclosure in it? I leave the answer to your Ladyship.'

'Isabel Miller is as incapable of an act of theft as I am. There is my answer, Mr Troy.'

The lawyer bowed resignedly, and advanced to the door.

'Am I to take your Ladyship's generous assertion as finally disposing of the question of the lost bank-note?' he inquired.

Lady Lydiard met the challenge without shrinking from it.

'No!' she said. 'The loss of the bank-note is known out of my house. Other persons may suspect this innocent girl as you suspect her. It is due to Isabel's reputation – her unstained reputation, Mr Troy! – that she should know what has happened, and should have an opportunity of defending herself. She is in the next room, Moody. Bring her here.'

Robert's courage failed him: he trembled at the bare idea of exposing Isabel to the terrible ordeal that awaited her. 'Oh, my Lady!' he pleaded, 'think again before you tell the poor girl that she is suspected of theft. Keep it a secret from her – the shame of it will break her heart!'

'Keep it a secret,' said Lady Lydiard, 'when the Rector and the Rector's wife both know of it! Do you think they will let the matter rest where it is, even if I could consent to hush it up? I must write to them; and I can't write anonymously after what has happened. Put yourself in Isabel's place, and tell me if you would thank the person who knew you to be innocently exposed to a disgraceful suspicion, and who concealed it from you? Go, Moody! The longer you delay, the harder it will be.'

With his head sunk on his breast, with anguish written in every line of his face, Moody obeyed. Passing slowly down the short passage which connected the two rooms, and still shrinking from the duty that had been imposed on him, he paused, looking through the curtains which hung over the entrance to the boudoir.

CHAPTER VII

The sight that met Moody's view wrung him to the heart.

Isabel and the dog were at play together. Among the varied accomplishments possessed by Tommie, the capacity to take his part at a game of hide-and-seek was one. His playfellow for the time being put a shawl or a handkerchief over his head, so as to prevent him from seeing, and then hid among the furniture a pocket-book, or a cigar-case, or a purse, or anything else that happened to be at hand, leaving the dog to find it, with his keen sense of smell to guide him. Doubly relieved by the fit and the bleeding, Tommie's spirits had revived; and he and Isabel had just begun their game when Moody looked into the room, charged with his terrible errand. 'You're burning, Tommie, you're burning!' cried the girl, laughing and clapping her hands. The next moment she happened to look round and saw Moody through the parted curtains. His face warned her instantly that something serious had happened. She advanced a few steps, her eyes resting on him in silent alarm. He was himself too painfully agitated to speak. Not a word was exchanged between Lady Lydiard and Mr Troy in the next room. In the complete stillness that prevailed, the dog was heard sniffing and fidgeting about the furniture. Robert took Isabel by the hand and led her into the drawing-room. 'For God's sake, spare her, my Lady!' he whispered. The lawyer heard him. 'No,' said Mr Troy. 'Be merciful, and tell her the truth!'

He spoke to a woman who stood in no need of his advice. The inherent nobility in Lady Lydiard's nature was aroused: her great heart offered itself patiently to any sorrow, to any sacrifice.

Putting her arm round Isabel – half caressing her, half supporting her – Lady Lydiard accepted the whole responsibility and told the whole truth.

Reeling under the first shock, the poor girl recovered herself with admirable courage. She raised her head, and eyed the lawyer without uttering a word. In its artless consciousness of innocence the look was nothing less than sublime. Addressing herself to Mr Troy, Lady Lydiard pointed to Isabel. 'Do you see guilt there?' she asked.

Mr Troy made no answer. In the melancholy experience of humanity to which his profession condemned him, he had seen conscious guilt assume the face of innocence, and helpless innocence admit the disguise of guilt: the keenest observation, in either case, failing completely to detect the truth. Lady Lydiard misinterpreted his silence as expressing the sullen self-assertion of a heartless man. She turned from him, in contempt, and held out her hand to Isabel.

'Mr Troy is not satisfied yet,' she said bitterly. 'My love, take my hand, and look me in the face as your equal; I know no difference of rank at such a time as this. Before God, who hears you, are you innocent of the theft of the bank-note?'

'Before God, who hears me,' Isabel answered, 'I am innocent.'

Lady Lydiard looked once more at the lawyer, and waited to hear if he believed *that*.

Mr Troy took refuge in dumb diplomacy – he made a low bow. It might have meant that he believed Isabel, or it might have meant that he modestly withdrew his own opinion into the background. Lady Lydiard did not condescend to inquire what it meant.

'The sooner we bring this painful scene to an end the better,' she said. 'I shall be glad to avail myself of your professional assistance, Mr Troy, within certain limits. Outside of my house, I beg that you will spare no trouble in tracing the lost money to the person who has really stolen it. Inside of my house, I must positively request that the disappearance of the note may never be alluded to, in any way whatever, until your inquiries have been successful in discovering the thief. In the meanwhile, Mrs Tollmidge and her family must not be sufferers by my loss: I shall pay the money again.' She paused, and pressed Isabel's hand with affectionate fervour. 'My child,' she said, 'one last word to you, and I have done. You remain here, with my trust in you, and my love for you, absolutely unshaken. When you think of what has been said here to-day, never forget that.'

Isabel bent her head, and kissed the kind hand that still held hers. The high spirit that was in her, inspired by Lady Lydiard's example, rose equal to the dreadful situation in which she was placed.

'No, my Lady,' she said calmly and sadly; 'it cannot be. What this gentleman has said of me is not to be denied – the appearances are against me. The letter was open, and I was alone in the room with it, and Mr Moody told me that a valuable inclosure was inside it. Dear and kind mistress! I am not fit to be a member of your household, I am not worthy to live with the honest people who serve you, while my innocence is in doubt. It is enough for me now that *you* don't doubt it. I can wait patiently, after that, for the day that gives me back my good name. Oh, my Lady, don't cry about it! Pray, pray don't cry!'

Lady Lydiard's self-control failed her for the first time. Isabel's courage had made Isabel dearer to her than ever. She sank into a chair, and covered her face with her handkerchief. Mr Troy turned aside abruptly, and examined a Japanese vase, without any idea in his mind of what he was looking at. Lady Lydiard had gravely misjudged him in believing him to be a heartless man.

Isabel followed the lawyer, and touched him gently on the arm to rouse his attention.

'I have one relation living, sir – an aunt – who will receive me if I go to her,' she said simply. 'Is there any harm in my going? Lady Lydiard will give you the address when you want me. Spare her Ladyship, sir, all the pain and trouble that you can.'

At last the heart that was in Mr Troy asserted itself. 'You are a fine creature!' he said, with a burst of enthusiasm. 'I agree with Lady Lydiard – I believe you are innocent, too; and I will leave no effort untried to find the proof of it' He turned aside again, and had another look at the Japanese vase.

As the lawyer withdrew himself from observation, Moody approached Isabel.

Thus far he had stood apart, watching her and listening to her in silence. Not a look that had crossed her face, not a word that had fallen from her, had escaped him. Unconsciously on her side, unconsciously on his side, she now wrought on his nature with a purifying and ennobling influence which animated it with a new life. All that had been selfish and violent in his passion for her left him to return no more. The immeasurable devotion which he laid at her feet, in the days that were yet to come – the unyielding courage which cheerfully accepted the sacrifice of himself when events demanded it at a later period of his life – struck root in him now. Without attempting to conceal the tears that were falling fast over his cheeks – striving vainly to express those new thoughts in him that were beyond the reach of words – he stood before her the truest friend and servant that ever woman had. 'Oh, my dear! my heart is heavy for you. Take me to serve you and help you. Her Ladyship's kindness will permit it, I am sure.'

He could say no more. In those simple words the cry of his heart reached her. 'Forgive me, Robert,' she answered, gratefully, 'if I said anything to pain you when we spoke together a little while since. I didn't mean it.' She gave him her hand, and looked timidly over her shoulder at Lady Lydiard. 'Let me go!' she said, in low, broken tones, 'Let me go!'

Mr Troy heard her, and stepped forward to interfere before Lady Lydiard could speak. The man had recovered his self-control; the lawyer took his place again on the scene.

'You must not leave us, my dear,' he said to Isabel, 'until I have put a question to Mr Moody in which you are interested. Do you happen to have the number of the lost bank-note?' he asked, turning to the steward.

Moody produced his slip of paper with the number on it. Mr Troy made two copies of it before he returned the paper. One copy he put in his pocket, the other he handed to Isabel.

'Keep it carefully,' he said. 'Neither you nor I know how soon it may be of use to you.'

Receiving the copy from him, she felt mechanically in her apron for her pocket-book. She had used it, in playing with the dog, as an object to hide from him; but she had suffered, and was still suffering, too keenly to be capable of the effort of remembrance. Moody, eager to help her even in the most trifling thing, guessed what had happened. 'You were playing with Tommie,' he said; 'is it in the next room?'

The dog heard his name pronounced through the open door. The next moment he trotted into the drawing-room with Isabel's pocket-book in his mouth. He was a strong, well-grown Scotch terrier of the largest size, with bright, intelligent eyes, and a coat of thick curling white hair, diversified by two light brown patches on his back. As he reached the middle of the room, and looked from one to another of the persons present, the fine sympathy of his race told him that there was trouble among his human friends. His tail dropped; he whined softly as he approached Isabel, and laid her pocket-book at her feet.

She knelt as she picked up the pocket-book, and raised her play-fellow of happier days to take her leave of him. As the dog put his paws on her shoulders, returning her caress, her first tears fell. 'Foolish of me,' she said, faintly, 'to cry over a dog. I can't help it. Good-by, Tommie!'

Putting him away from her gently, she walked towards the door. The dog instantly followed. She put him away from her, for the second time, and left him. He was not to be denied; he followed her again, and took the skirt of her dress in his teeth, as if to hold her back. Robert forced the dog, growling and resisting with all his might, to let go of the dress. 'Don't be rough with him,' said Isabel. 'Put him on her ladyship's lap; he will be quieter there.' Robert obeyed. He whispered to Lady Lydiard as she received the dog: she seemed to be still incapable of speaking – she bowed her head in silent assent. Robert hurried back to Isabel before she had passed the door. 'Not alone!' he said entreatingly. 'Her Ladyship permits it, Isabel. Let me see you safe to your aunt's house.'

Isabel looked at him, felt for him, and yielded.

'Yes,' she answered softly; 'to make amends for what I said to you when I was thoughtless and happy!' She waited a little to compose herself before she spoke her farewell words to Lady Lydiard. 'Good-bye, my Lady. Your kindness has not been thrown away on an ungrateful girl. I love you, and thank you, with all my heart.'

Lady Lydiard rose, placing the dog on the chair as she left it. She seemed to have grown older by years, instead of by minutes, in the short interval that had passed since she had hidden her face from view. 'I can't bear it!' she cried, in husky, broken tones. 'Isabel! Isabel! I forbid you to leave me!'

But one person could venture to resist her. That person was Mr Troy – and Mr Troy knew it.

'Control yourself,' he said to her in a whisper. 'The girl is doing what is best and most becoming in her position – and is doing it with a patience and courage wonderful to see. She places herself under the protection of her nearest relative, until her character is vindicated and her position in your house is once more beyond a doubt. Is this a time to throw obstacles in her way? Be worthy of yourself, Lady Lydiard – and think of the day when she will return to you without the breath of a suspicion to rest on her!'

There was no disputing with him – he was too plainly in the right. Lady Lydiard submitted; she concealed the torture that her own resolution inflicted on her with an endurance which was, indeed, worthy of herself. Taking Isabel in her arms she kissed her in a passion of sorrow and love. 'My poor dear! My own sweet girl! don't suppose that this is a parting kiss! I shall see you again – often and often I shall see you again at your aunt's!' At a sign from Mr Troy, Robert took Isabel's arm in his and led her away. Tommie, watching her from his chair, lifted his little white muzzle as his play-fellow looked back on passing the doorway. The long, melancholy, farewell howl of the dog was the last sound Isabel Miller heard as she left the house.

PART THE SECOND

THE DISCOVERY

CHAPTER VIII

On the day after Isabel's departure, diligent Mr Troy set forth for the Head Office in Whitehall to consult the police on the question of the missing money. He had previously sent information of the robbery to the Bank of England, and had also advertised the loss in the daily newspapers.

The air was so pleasant, and the sun was so bright, that he determined on proceeding to his destination on foot. He was hardly out of sight of his own offices when he was overtaken by a friend, who was also walking in the direction of Whitehall. This gentleman was a person of considerable worldly wisdom and experience; he had been officially associated with cases of striking and notorious crime, in which Government had lent its assistance to discover and punish the criminals. The opinion of a person in this position might be of the greatest value to Mr Troy, whose practice as a solicitor had thus far never brought him into collision with thieves and mysteries. He accordingly decided, in Isabel's interests, on confiding to his friend the nature of his errand to the police. Concealing the name, but concealing nothing else, he described what had happened on the previous day at Lady Lydiard's house, and then put the question plainly to his companion.

'What would you do in my place?'

'In your place,' his friend answered quietly, 'I should not waste time and money in consulting the police.'

'Not consult the police!' exclaimed Mr Troy in amazement. 'Surely, I have not made myself understood? I am going to the Head Office; and I have got a letter of introduction to the chief inspector in the detective department. I am afraid I omitted to mention that?'

'It doesn't make any difference,' proceeded the other, as coolly as ever. 'You have asked for my advice, and I give you my advice. Tear up your letter of introduction, and don't stir a step farther in the direction of Whitehall.'

Mr Troy began to understand. 'You don't believe in the detective police?' he said.

'Who *can* believe in them, who reads his newspaper and remembers what he reads?' his friend rejoined. 'Fortunately for the detective department, the public in general forgets what it reads. Go to your club, and look at the criminal history of our own time, recorded in the newspapers. Every crime is more or less a mystery. You will see that the mysteries which the police discover are, almost without exception, mysteries made penetrable by the commonest capacity, through the extraordinary stupidity exhibited in the means taken to hide the crime. On the other hand, let the guilty man or woman be a resolute and intelligent person, capable of setting his (or her) wits fairly against the wits of the police – in other words, let the mystery really *be* a mystery – and cite me a case if you can (a really difficult and perplexing case) in which the criminal has not escaped. Mind! I don't charge the police with neglecting their work. No doubt they do their best, and take the greatest pains in following the routine to which they have been trained. It is their misfortune, not their fault, that there is no man of superior intelligence among them – I mean no man who is capable, in great emergencies, of placing himself above conventional methods, and following a new way of his own. There have been such men in the police – men naturally endowed with that faculty of mental analysis which can decompose a mystery, resolve it into its component parts, and find the clue at the bottom, no matter how remote from ordinary observation it may be. But those men have died, or have retired. One of them would have been invaluable to you in the case you have just mentioned to me. As things are, unless you are wrong in believing in the young lady's innocence, the person who has stolen that bank-note will be no easy person to find. In my opinion, there is only one man now in London who is likely to be of the slightest assistance to you – and he is not in the police.'

'Who is he?' asked Mr Troy.

'An old rogue, who was once in your branch of the legal profession,' the friend answered. 'You may, perhaps, remember the name: they call him "Old Sharon".'

'What! The scoundrel who was struck off the Roll of Attorneys, years since? Is he still alive?'

'Alive and prospering. He lives in a court or lane running out of Long-acre, and he offers advice to persons interested in recovering missing objects of any sort. Whether you have lost your wife, or lost your cigar-case, Old Sharon is equally useful to you. He has an inbred capacity for reading the riddle the right way in cases of mystery, great or small. In short, he possesses exactly that analytical faculty to which I alluded just now. I have his address at my office, if you think it worth while to try him.'

'Who can trust such a man?' Mr Troy objected. 'He would be sure to deceive me.'

'You are entirely mistaken. Since he was struck off the Rolls Old Sharon has discovered that the straight way is, on the whole, the best way, even in a man's own interests. His consultation fee is a guinea; and he gives a signed estimate beforehand for any supplementary expenses that may follow. I can tell you (this is, of course, strictly between ourselves) that the authorities at my office took his advice in a Government case that puzzled the police. We approached him, of course, through persons who were to be trusted to represent us, without betraying the source from which their instructions were derived; and we found the old rascal's advice well worth paying for. It is quite likely that he may not succeed so well in your case. Try the police, by all means; and, if they fail, why, there is Sharon as a last resort.'

This arrangement commended itself to Mr Troy's professional caution. He went on to Whitehall, and he tried the detective police. They at once adopted the obvious conclusion to persons of ordinary capacity – the conclusion that Isabel was the thief.

Acting on this conviction, the authorities sent an experienced woman from the office to Lady Lydiard's house, to examine the poor girl's clothes and ornaments before they were packed up and sent after her to her aunt's. The search led to nothing. The only objects of any value that were discovered had been presents from Lady Lydiard. No jewellers' or milliners' bills were among the papers found in her desk. Not a sign of secret extravagance in dress was to be seen anywhere. Defeated so far, the police proposed next to have Isabel privately watched. There might be a prodigal lover somewhere in the background, with ruin staring him in the face unless he could raise five hundred pounds. Lady Lydiard (who had only consented to the search under stress of persuasive argument from Mr Troy) resented this ingenious idea as an insult. She declared that if Isabel was watched the girl should know of it instantly from her own lips. The police listened with perfect resignation and decorum, and politely shifted their ground. A certain suspicion (they remarked) always rested in cases of this sort on the servants. Would her Ladyship object to private inquiries into the characters and proceedings of the servants? Her Ladyship instantly objected, in the most positive terms. Thereupon the 'Inspector' asked for a minute's private conversation with Mr Troy. 'The thief is certainly a member of Lady Lydiard's household,' this functionary remarked, in his politely-positive way. 'If her Ladyship persists in refusing to let us make the necessary inquiries, our hands are tied, and the case comes to an end through no fault of ours. If her Ladyship changes her mind, perhaps you will drop me a line, sir, to that effect. Good morning.'

So the experiment of consulting the police came to an untimely end. The one result obtained was the expression of purblind opinion by the authorities of the detective department, which pointed to Isabel, or to one of the servants, as the undiscovered thief. Thinking the matter over in the retirement of his own office – and not forgetting his promise to Isabel to leave no means untried of establishing her innocence – Mr Troy could see but one alternative left to him. He took up his pen, and wrote to his friend at the Government office. There was nothing for it now but to run the risk, and try Old Sharon.

CHAPTER IX

The next day, Mr Troy (taking Robert Moody with him as a valuable witness) rang the bell at the mean and dirty lodging-house in which Old Sharon received the clients who stood in need of his advice.

They were led up stairs to a back room on the second floor of the house. Entering the room, they discovered through a thick cloud of tobacco smoke, a small, fat, baldheaded, dirty, old man, in an arm-chair, robed in a tattered flannel dressing-gown, with a short pipe in his mouth, a pug-dog on his lap, and a French novel in his hands.

'Is it business?' asked Old Sharon, speaking in a hoarse, asthmatical voice, and fixing a pair of bright, shameless, black eyes attentively on the two visitors.

'It *is* business,' Mr Troy answered, looking at the old rogue who had disgraced an honourable profession, as he might have looked at a reptile which had just risen rampant at his feet. 'What is your fee for a consultation?'

'You give me a guinea, and I'll give you half an hour.' With this reply Old Sharon held out his unwashed hand across the rickety ink-splashed table at which he was sitting.

Mr Troy would not have touched him with the tips of his own fingers for a thousand pounds. He laid the guinea on the table.

Old Sharon burst into a fierce laugh – a laugh strangely accompanied by a frowning contraction of his eyebrows, and a frightful exhibition of the whole inside of his mouth. 'I'm not clean enough for you – eh?' he said, with an appearance of being very much amused. 'There's a dirty old man described in this book that is a little like me.' He held up his French novel. 'Have you read it? A capital story – well put together. Ah, you haven't read it? You have got a pleasure to come. I say, do you mind tobacco-smoke? I think faster while I smoke – that's all.'

Mr Troy's respectable hand waved a silent permission to smoke, given under dignified protest.

'All right,' said Old Sharon. 'Now, get on.'

He laid himself back in his chair, and puffed out his smoke, with eyes lazily half closed, like the eyes of the pug-dog on his lap. At that moment, indeed, there was a curious resemblance between the two. They both seemed to be preparing themselves, in the same idle way, for the same comfortable nap.

Mr Troy stated the circumstances under which the five-hundred-pound note had disappeared, in clear and consecutive narrative. When he had done, Old Sharon suddenly opened his eyes. The pug-dog suddenly opened his eyes. Old Sharon looked hard at Mr Troy. The pug looked hard at Mr Troy. Old Sharon spoke. The pug growled.

'I know who you are – you're a lawyer. Don't be alarmed! I never saw you before; and I don't know your name. What I do know is a lawyer's statement of facts when I hear it. Who's this?' Old Sharon looked inquisitively at Moody as he put the question.

Mr Troy introduced Moody as a competent witness, thoroughly acquainted with the circumstances, and ready and willing to answer any questions relating to them. Old Sharon waited a little, smoking hard and thinking hard. 'Now, then!' he burst out in his fiercely sudden way. 'I'm going to get to the root of the matter.'

He leaned forward with his elbows on the table, and began his examination of Moody. Heartily as Mr Troy despised and disliked the old rogue, he listened with astonishment and admiration – literally extorted from him by the marvellous ability with which the questions were adapted to the end in view. In a quarter of an hour Old Sharon had extracted from the witness everything, literally everything down to the smallest detail, that Moody could tell him. Having now, in his own phrase, 'got to the root of the matter', he relit his pipe with a grunt of satisfaction, and laid himself back in his old arm-chair.

'Well?' said Mr Troy. 'Have you formed your opinion?'

'Yes; I've formed my opinion.'

'What is it?'

Instead of replying, Old Sharon winked confidentially at Mr Troy, and put a question on his side.

'I say! is a ten-pound note much of an object to you?'

'It depends on what the money is wanted for,' answered Mr Troy.

'Look here,' said Old Sharon; 'I give you an opinion for your guinea; but, mind this, it's an opinion founded on hearsay – and you know as a lawyer what that is worth. Venture your ten pounds – in plain English, pay me for my time and trouble in a baffling and difficult case – and I'll give you an opinion founded on my own experience.'

'Explain yourself a little more clearly,' said Mr Troy. 'What do you guarantee to tell us if we venture the ten pounds?'

'I guarantee to name the person, or the persons, on whom the suspicion really rests. And if you employ me after that, I guarantee (before you pay me a halfpenny more) to prove that I am right by laying my hand on the thief.'

'Let us have the guinea opinion first,' said Mr Troy.

Old Sharon made another frightful exhibition of the whole inside of his mouth; his laugh was louder and fiercer than ever. 'I like you!' he said to Mr Troy, 'you are so devilish fond of your money. Lord! how rich you must be! Now listen. Here's the guinea opinion: – Suspect, in this case, the very last person on whom suspicion could possibly fall.'

Moody, listening attentively, started, and changed colour at those last words. Mr Troy looked thoroughly disappointed and made no attempt to conceal it.

'Is that all?' he asked.

'All?' retorted the cynical vagabond. 'You're a pretty lawyer! What more can I say, when I don't know for certain whether the witness who has given me my information has misled me or not? Have I spoken to the girl and formed my own opinion? No! Have I been introduced among the servants (as errand-boy, or to clean the boots and shoes, or what not), and have I formed my own judgement of *them*? No! I take your opinions for granted, and I tell you how I should set to work myself if they were *my* opinions too – and that's a guinea's-worth, a devilish good guinea's-worth to a rich man like you!'

Old Sharon's logic produced a certain effect on Mr Troy, in spite of himself. It was smartly put from his point of view – there was no denying that.

'Even if I consented to your proposal,' he said, 'I should object to your annoying the young lady with impertinent questions, or to your being introduced as a spy into a respectable house.'

Old Sharon doubled his dirty fists and drummed with them on the rickety table in a comical frenzy of impatience while Mr Troy was speaking.

'What the devil do you know about my way of doing my business?' he burst out when the lawyer had done. 'One of us two is talking like a born idiot – and (mind this) it isn't me. Look here! Your young lady goes out for a walk, and she meets with a dirty, shabby old beggar – I look like a shabby old beggar already, don't I? Very good. This dirty old wretch whines and whimpers and tells a long story, and gets sixpence out of the girl – and knows her by that time, inside and out, as well as if he had made her – and, mark! hasn't asked her a single question, and, instead of annoying her, has made her happy in the performance of a charitable action. Stop a bit! I haven't done with you yet. Who blacks your boots and shoes? Look here!' He pushed his pug-dog off his lap, dived under the table, appeared again with an old boot and a bottle of blackening, and set to work with tigerish activity. 'I'm going out for a walk, you know, and I may as well make myself smart.' With that announcement, he began to sing over his work – a song of sentiment, popular in England in the early part of the present century – 'She's all my fancy painted her; she's lovely, she's divine; but her heart it is another's; and it never can be mine! Too-ral-loo-ral-loo. I like a love song. Brush away! brush away! till I see my own pretty face in the blacking. Hey! Here's a nice, harmless, jolly old man! sings and jokes over his work, and makes the kitchen quite cheerful. What's that you say? He's a stranger, and don't talk to him too freely. You ought to be ashamed of yourself to speak in that way of a poor old fellow with one foot in the grave. Mrs-cook will give him a nice bit of dinner in the scullery; and John-footman will look out an old coat for him. And when he's heard everything he wants to hear, and doesn't come back again the next day to his work – what do they think of it in the servants' hall? Do they say, "We've had a spy among us!" Yah! you know better than that, by this time. The cheerful old man has been run over in the street, or is down with the fever, or has turned up his toes in the parish dead-house – that's what they say in the servants' hall. Try me in your own kitchen, and see if your servants take me for a spy. Come, come, Mr Lawyer! out with your ten pounds, and don't waste any more precious time about it!'

'I will consider and let you know,' said Mr Troy.

Old Sharon laughed more ferociously than ever, and hobbled round the table in a great hurry to the place at which Moody was sitting. He laid one hand on the steward's shoulder, and pointed derisively with the other to Mr Troy.

'I say, Mr Silent-man! Bet you five pounds I never hear of that lawyer again!'

Silently attentive all through the interview (except when he was answering questions), Moody only replied in the fewest words. 'I don't bet,' was all he said. He showed no resentment at Sharon's familiarity, and he appeared to find no amusement in Sharon's extraordinary talk. The old vagabond seemed actually to produce a serious impression on him! When Mr Troy set the example of rising to go, he still kept his seat, and looked at the lawyer as if he regretted leaving the atmosphere of tobacco-smoke reeking in the dirty room.

'Have you anything to say before we go?' Mr Troy asked.

Moody rose slowly and looked at Old Sharon. 'Not just now, sir,' he replied, looking away again, after a moment's reflection.

Old Sharon interpreted Moody's look and Moody's reply from his own peculiar point of view. He suddenly drew the steward away into a corner of the room.

'I say!' he began, in a whisper. 'Upon your solemn word of honour, you know – are you as rich as the lawyer there?'

'Certainly not.'

'Look here! It's half price to a poor man. If you feel like coming back, on your own account – five pounds will do from *you*. There! there! Think of it! – think of it!'

'Now, then!' said Mr Troy, waiting for his companion, with the door open in his hand. He looked back at Sharon when Moody joined him. The old vagabond was settled again in his arm-chair, with his dog in his lap; his pipe in his mouth, and his French novel in his hand; exhibiting exactly the picture of frowsy comfort which he had presented when his visitors first entered the room.

'Good-day,' said Mr Troy, with haughty condescension.

'Don't interrupt me!' rejoined Old Sharon, absorbed in his novel. 'You've had your guinea's worth. Lord! what a lovely book this is! Don't interrupt me!'

'Impudent scoundrel!' said Mr Troy, when he and Moody were in the street again. 'What could my friend mean by recommending him? Fancy his expecting me to trust him with ten pounds! I consider even the guinea completely thrown away.'

'Begging your pardon, sir,' said Moody, 'I don't quite agree with you there.'

'What! you don't mean to tell me you understand that oracular sentence of his – "Suspect the very last person on whom suspicion could possibly fall." Rubbish!'

'I don't say I understand it, sir. I only say it has set me thinking.'

'Thinking of what? Do your suspicions point to the thief?'

'If you will please to excuse me, Mr Troy, I should like to wait a while before I answer that.'

Mr Troy suddenly stood still, and eyed his companion a little distrustfully.

'Are you going to turn detective policeman on your own account?' he asked.

'There's nothing I won't turn to, and try, to help Miss Isabel in this matter,' Moody answered firmly. 'I have saved a few hundred pounds in Lady Lydiard's service, and I am ready to spend every farthing of it, if I can only discover the thief.'

Mr Troy walked on again. 'Miss Isabel seems to have a good friend in you,' he said. He was (perhaps unconsciously) a little offended by the independent tone in which the steward spoke, after he had himself engaged to take the vindication of the girl's innocence into his own hands.

'Miss Isabel has a devoted servant and slave in me!' Moody answered, with passionate enthusiasm.

'Very creditable; I haven't a word to say against it,' Mr Troy rejoined. 'But don't forget that the young lady has other devoted friends besides you. I am her devoted friend, for instance – I have promised to serve her, and I mean to keep my word. You will excuse me for adding that my experience and discretion are quite as likely to be useful to her as your enthusiasm. I know the world well enough to be careful in trusting strangers. It will do you no harm, Mr Moody, to follow my example.'

Moody accepted his reproof with becoming patience and resignation. 'If you have anything to propose, sir, that will be of service to Miss Isabel,' he said, 'I shall be happy if I can assist you in the humblest capacity.'

'And if not?' Mr Troy inquired, conscious of having nothing to propose as he asked the question.

'In that case, sir, I must take my own course, and blame nobody but myself if it leads me astray.'

Mr Troy said no more: he parted from Moody at the next turning.

Pursuing the subject privately in his own mind, he decided on taking the earliest opportunity of visiting Isabel at her aunt's house, and on warning her, in her future intercourse with Moody, not to trust too much to the steward's discretion. 'I haven't a doubt,' thought the lawyer, 'of what he means to do next. The infatuated fool is going back to Old Sharon!'

CHAPTER X

Returning to his office, Mr Troy discovered, among the correspondence that was waiting for him, a letter from the very person whose welfare was still the uppermost subject in his mind. Isabel Miller wrote in these terms:

'Dear Sir, – My aunt, Miss Pink, is very desirous of consulting you professionally at the earliest opportunity. Although South Morden is within little more than half an hour's railway ride from London, Miss Pink does not presume to ask you to visit her, being well aware of the value of your time. Will you, therefore, be so kind as to let me know when it will be convenient to you to receive my aunt at your office in London? Believe me, dear Sir, respectfully yours, ISABEL MILLER P.S. – I am further instructed to say that the regrettable event at Lady Lydiard's house is the proposed subject of the consultation. The Lawn, South Morden. Thursday.'

Mr Troy smiled as he read the letter. 'Too formal for a young girl!' he said to himself. 'Every word of it has been dictated by Miss Pink.' He was not long in deciding what course he should take. There was a pressing necessity for cautioning Isabel, and here was his opportunity. He sent for his head clerk, and looked at his list of engagements for the day. There was nothing set down in the book which the clerk was not quite as well able to do as the master. Mr Troy consulted his railway-guide, ordered his cab, and caught the next train to South Morden.

South Morden was then (and remains to this day) one of those primitive agricultural villages, passed over by the march of modern progress, which are still to be found in the near neighbourhood of London. Only the slow trains stopped at the station; and there was so little to do that the station-master and his porter grew flowers on the embankment, and trained creepers over the waiting-room window. Turning your back on the railway, and walking along the one street of South Morden, you found yourself in the old England of two centuries since. Gabled cottages, with fast-closed windows; pigs and poultry in quiet possession of the road; the venerable church surrounded by its shady burial-ground; the grocer's shop which sold everything, and the butcher's shop which sold nothing; the scarce inhabitants who liked a good look at a stranger, and the unwashed children who were pictures of dirty health; the clash of the iron-chained bucket in the public well, and the thump of the falling ninepins in the skittle-ground behind the public-house; the horse-pond on the one bit of open ground, and the old elm-tree with the wooden seat round it on the other – these were some of the objects that you saw, and some of the noises that you heard in South Morden, as you passed from one end of the village to the other.

About half a mile beyond the last of the old cottages, modern England met you again under the form of a row of little villas, set up by an adventurous London builder who had bought the land a bargain. Each villa stood in its own little garden, and looked across a stony road at the meadow lands and softly-rising wooded hills beyond. Each villa faced you in the sunshine with the horrid glare of new red brick, and forced its nonsensical name on your attention, traced in bright paint on the posts of its entrance gate. Consulting the posts as he advanced, Mr Troy arrived in due course of time at the villa called The Lawn, which derived its name apparently from a circular patch of grass in front of the house. The gate resisting his efforts to open it, he rang the bell.

Admitted by a trim, clean, shy little maid-servant, Mr Troy looked about him in amazement. Turn which way he might, he found himself silently confronted by posted and painted instructions to visitors, which forbade him to do this, and commanded him to do that, at every step of his progress from the gate to the house. On the side of the lawn a label informed him that he was not to walk on the grass. On the other side a painted hand pointed along a boundary-wall to an inscription which warned him to go that way if he had business in the kitchen. On the gravel walk at the foot of the house-steps words, neatly traced in little white shells, reminded him not to 'forget the scraper'. On the door-step he was informed, in letters of lead, that he was 'Welcome!'. On the mat in the passage bristly black words burst on his attention, commanding him to 'wipe his shoes'. Even the hat-stand in the hall was not allowed to speak for itself: it had 'Hats and Cloaks' inscribed on it, and it issued its directions imperatively in the matter of your wet umbrella – 'Put it here!'

Giving the trim little servant his card, Mr Troy was introduced to a reception-room on the lower floor. Before he had time to look round him the door was opened again from without, and Isabel stole into the room on tiptoe. She looked worn and anxious. When she shook hands with the old lawyer the charming smile that he remembered so well was gone.

'Don't say you have seen me,' she whispered. 'I am not to come into the room till my aunt sends for me. Tell me two things before I run away again. How is Lady Lydiard? And have you discovered the thief?'

'Lady Lydiard was well when I last saw her; and we have not yet succeeded in discovering the thief.' Having answered the questions in those terms, Mr Troy decided on cautioning Isabel on the subject of the steward while he had the chance. 'One question on my side,' he said, holding her back from the door by the arm. 'Do you expect Moody to visit you here?'

'I am *sure* he will visit me,' Isabel answered warmly. 'He has promised to come here at my request. I never knew what a kind heart Robert Moody had till this misfortune fell on me.

My aunt, who is not easily taken with strangers, respects and admires him. I can't tell you how good he was to me on the journey here – and how kindly, how nobly, he spoke to me when we parted.' She paused, and turned her head away. The tears were rising in her eyes. 'In my situation,' she said faintly, 'kindness is very keenly felt. Don't notice me, Mr Troy.'

The lawyer waited a moment to let her recover herself.

'I agree entirely, my dear, in your opinion of Moody,' he said. 'At the same time, I think it right to warn you that his zeal in your service may possibly outrun his discretion. He may feel too confidently about penetrating the mystery of the missing money; and, unless you are on your guard, he may raise false hopes in you when you next see him. Listen to any advice that he may give you, by all means. But, before you decide on being guided by his opinion, consult my older experience, and hear what I have to say on the subject. Don't suppose that I am attempting to make you distrust this good friend,' he added, noticing the look of uneasy surprise which Isabel fixed on him. 'No such idea is in my mind. I only warn you that Moody's eagerness to be of service to you may mislead him. You understand me.'

'Yes, sir,' replied Isabel coldly; 'I understand you. Please let me go now. My aunt will be down directly; and she must not find me here.' She curtseyed with distant respect, and left the room.

'So much for trying to put two ideas together into a girl's mind!' thought Mr Troy, when he was alone again. 'The little fool evidently thinks I am jealous of Moody's place in her estimation. Well! I have done my duty – and I can do no more.'

He looked round the room. Not a chair was out of its place, not a speck of dust was to be seen. The brightly-perfect polish of the table made your eyes ache; the ornaments on it looked as if they had never been touched by mortal hand; the piano was an object for distant admiration, not an instrument to be played on; the carpet made Mr Troy look nervously at the soles of his shoes; and the sofa (protected by layers of white crochet-work) said as plainly as if in words, 'Sit on me if you dare!' Mr Troy retreated to a bookcase at the farther end of the room. The books fitted the shelves to such absolute perfection that he had some difficulty in taking one of them out. When he had succeeded, he found himself in possession of a volume of the History of England. On the fly-leaf he encountered another written warning: – 'This book belongs to Miss Pink's Academy for Young Ladies, and is not to be removed from the library.' The date, which was added, referred to a period of ten years since. Miss Pink now stood revealed as a retired schoolmistress; and Mr Troy began to understand some of the characteristic peculiarities of that lady's establishment which had puzzled him up to the present time.

He had just succeeded in putting the book back again when the door opened once more, and Isabel's aunt entered the room.

If Miss Pink could, by any possible conjuncture of circumstances, have disappeared mysteriously from her house and her friends, the police would have found the greatest difficulty in composing the necessary description of the missing lady. The acutest observer could have discovered nothing that was noticeable or characteristic in her personal appearance. The pen of the present writer portrays her in despair by a series of negatives. She was not young, she was not old; she was neither tall nor short, nor stout nor thin; nobody could call her features attractive, and nobody could call them ugly; there was nothing in her voice, her expression, her manner, or her dress that differed in any appreciable degree from the voice, expression, manner, and dress of five hundred thousand other single ladies of her age and position in the world. If you had asked her to describe herself, she would have answered, 'I am a gentlewoman'; and if you had further inquired which of her numerous accomplishments took highest rank in her own esteem, she would have replied, 'My powers of conversation'. For the rest, she was Miss Pink, of South Morden; and, when that has been said, all has been said.

'Pray be seated, sir. We have had a beautiful day, after the long-continued wet weather. I am told that the season is very unfavourable for wall-fruit. May I offer you some refreshment after your journey?' In these terms and in the smoothest of voices, Miss Pink opened the interview.

Mr Troy made a polite reply, and added a few strictly conventional remarks on the beauty of the neighbourhood. Not even a lawyer could sit in Miss Pink's presence, and hear Miss Pink's conversation, without feeling himself called upon (in the nursery phrase) to 'be on his best behaviour'.

'It is extremely kind of you, Mr Troy, to favour me with this visit,' Miss Pink resumed. 'I am well aware that the time of professional gentlemen is of especial value to them; and I will therefore ask you to excuse me if I proceed abruptly to the subject on which I desire to consult your experience.'

Here the lady modestly smoothed out her dress over her knees, and the lawyer made a bow. Miss Pink's highly-trained conversation had perhaps one fault – it was not, strictly speaking, conversation at all. In its effect on her hearers it rather resembled the contents of a fluently conventional letter, read aloud.

'The circumstances under which my niece Isabel has left Lady Lydiard's house,' Miss Pink proceeded, 'are so indescribably painful – I will go further, I will say so deeply humiliating – that I have forbidden her to refer to them again in my presence, or to mention them in the future to any living creature besides myself. You are acquainted with those circumstances, Mr Troy; and you will understand my indignation when I first learnt that my sister's child had been suspected of theft. I have not the honour of being acquainted with Lady Lydiard. She is not a Countess, I believe? Just so! Her husband was only a Baron. I am not acquainted with Lady Lydiard; and I will not trust myself to say what I think of her conduct to my niece.'

'Pardon me, madam,' Mr Troy interposed. 'Before you say any more about Lady Lydiard, I really must beg leave to observe —— '

'Pardon *me*,' Miss Pink rejoined. 'I never form a hasty judgment. Lady Lydiard's conduct is beyond the reach of any defence, no matter how ingenious it may be. You may not be aware, sir, that in receiving my niece under her roof her Ladyship was receiving a gentlewoman by birth as well as by education. My late lamented sister was the daughter of a clergyman of the Church of England. I need hardly remind you that, as such, she was a born lady. Under favouring circumstances, Isabel's maternal grandfather might have been Archbishop of Canterbury, and have taken precedence of the

whole House of Peers, the Princes of the blood Royal alone
excepted. I am not prepared to say that my niece is equally
well connected on her father's side. My sister surprised – I will
not add shocked – us when she married a chemist. At the same
time, a chemist is not a tradesman. He is a gentleman at one
end of the profession of Medicine, and a titled physician is a
gentleman at the other end. That is all. In inviting Isabel to
reside with her, Lady Lydiard, I repeat, was bound to
remember that she was associating herself with a young
gentlewoman. She has *not* remembered this, which is one
insult; and she had suspected my niece of theft, which is
another.'

Miss Pink paused to take breath. Mr Troy made a second
attempt to get a hearing.

'Will you kindly permit me, madam, to say a few words?'

'No!' said Miss Pink, asserting the most immovable obstinacy under the blandest politeness of manner. 'Your time, Mr
Troy, is really too valuable! Not even your trained intellect
can excuse conduct which is manifestly *in*excusable on the face
of it. Now you know my opinion of Lady Lydiard, you will
not be surprised to hear that I decline to trust her Ladyship.
She may, or she may not, cause the necessary inquiries to be
made for the vindication of my niece's character. In a matter
so serious as this – I may say, in a duty which I owe to the
memories of my sister and my parents – I will not leave the
responsibility to Lady Lydiard. I will take it on myself. Let
me add that I am able to pay the necessary expenses. The
earlier years of my life, Mr Troy, have been passed in the
tuition of young ladies. I have been happy in meriting the
confidence of parents; and I have been strict in observing the
golden rules of economy. On my retirement, I have been able
to invest a modest, a very modest, little fortune in the Funds.
A portion of it is at the service of my niece for the recovery of
her good name; and I desire to place the necessary investigation confidentially, in your hands. You are acquainted with
the case; and the case naturally goes to you. I could not prevail
on myself – I really could not prevail on myself to mention it
to a stranger. That is the business on which I wished to consult
you. Please say nothing more about Lady Lydiard – the
subject is inexpressibly disagreeable to me. I will only trespass

on your kindness to tell me if I have succeeded in making myself understood.'

Miss Pink leaned back in her chair, at the exact angle permitted by the laws of propriety; rested her left elbow on the palm of her right hand, and lightly supported her cheek with her fore finger and thumb. In this position she waited Mr Troy's answer – the living picture of human obstinacy in its most respectable form.

If Mr Troy had not been a lawyer – in other words, if he had not been professionally capable of persisting in his own course, in the face of every conceivable difficulty and discouragement – Miss Pink might have remained in undisturbed possession of her own opinions. As it was, Mr Troy had got his hearing at last; and no matter how obstinately she might close her eyes to it, Miss Pink was now destined to have the other side of the case presented to her view.

'I am sincerely obliged to you, madam, for the expression of your confidence in me,' Mr Troy began; 'at the same time, I must beg you to excuse me if I decline to accept your proposal.'

Miss Pink had not expected to receive such an answer as this. The lawyer's brief refusal surprised and annoyed her.

'Why do you decline to assist me?' she asked.

'Because,' answered Mr Troy, 'my services are already engaged, in Miss Isabel's interest, by a client whom I have served for more than twenty years. My client is —— '

Miss Pink anticipated the coming disclosure. 'You need not trouble yourself, sir, to mention your client's name,' she said.

'My client,' persisted Mr Troy, 'loves Miss Isabel dearly —— '

'That is a matter of opinion,' Miss Pink interposed.

'And believes in Miss Isabel's innocence,' proceeded the irrepressible lawyer, 'as firmly as you believe in it yourself.'

Miss Pink (being human) had a temper; and Mr Troy had found his way to it.

'If Lady Lydiard believes in my niece's innocence,' said Miss Pink, suddenly sitting bolt upright in her chair, 'why has my niece been compelled, in justice to herself, to leave Lady Lydiard's house?'

'You will admit, madam,' Mr Troy answered cautiously, 'that we are all of us liable, in this wicked world, to be the victims of appearances. Your niece is a victim – an innocent victim. She wisely withdraws from Lady Lydiard's house until appearances are proved to be false and her position is cleared up.'

Miss Pink had her reply ready. 'That is simply acknowledging, in other words, that my niece is suspected. I am only a woman, Mr Troy – but it is not quite so easy to mislead me as you seem to suppose.'

Mr Troy's temper was admirably trained. But it began to acknowledge that Miss Pink's powers of irritation could sting to some purpose.

'No intention of misleading you, madam, has ever crossed my mind,' he rejoined warmly. 'As for your niece, I can tell you this. In all my experience of Lady Lydiard, I never saw her so distressed as she was when Miss Isabel left the house!'

'Indeed!' said Miss Pink, with an incredulous smile. 'In my rank of life, when we feel distressed about a person, we do our best to comfort that person by a kind letter or an early visit. But then I am not a lady of title.'

'Lady Lydiard engaged herself to call on Miss Isabel in my hearing,' said Mr Troy. 'Lady Lydiard is the most generous woman living!'

'Lady Lydiard is here!' cried a joyful voice on the other side of the door.

At the same moment, Isabel burst into the room in a state of excitement which actually ignored the formidable presence of Miss Pink. 'I beg your pardon, aunt! I was upstairs at the window, and I saw the carriage stop at the gate. And Tommie has come, too! The darling saw me at the window!' cried the poor girl, her eyes sparkling with delight as a perfect explosion of barking made itself heard over the tramp of horses' feet and the crash of carriage wheels outside.

Miss Pink rose slowly, with a dignity that looked capable of adequately receiving – not one noble lady only, but the whole peerage of England.

'Control yourself, dear Isabel,' she said. 'No well-bred young lady permits herself to become unduly excited. Stand by my side – a little behind me.'

Isabel obeyed. Mr Troy kept his place, and privately enjoyed his triumph over Miss Pink. If Lady Lydiard had been actually in league with him, she could not have chosen a more opportune time for her visit. A momentary interval passed. The carriage drew up at the door; the horses trampled on the gravel; the bell rung madly; the uproar of Tommie, released from the carriage and clamouring to be let in, redoubled its fury. Never before had such an unruly burst of noises invaded the tranquillity of Miss Pink's villa!

CHAPTER XI

The trim little maid-servant ran up stairs from the modest little kitchen, trembling at the terrible prospect of having to open the door. Miss Pink, deafened by the barking, had just time to say, 'What a very ill-behaved dog!' when a sound of small objects overthrown in the hall, and a scurrying of furious claws across the oil-cloth, announced that Tommie had invaded the house. As the servant appeared, introducing Lady Lydiard, the dog ran in. He made one frantic leap at Isabel, which would certainly have knocked her down but for the chair that happened to be standing behind her. Received on her lap, the faithful creature half-smothered her with his caresses. He barked, he shrieked, in his joy at seeing her again. He jumped off her lap and tore round and round the room at the top of his speed; and every time he passed Miss Pink he showed the whole range of his teeth and snarled ferociously at her ankles. Having at last exhausted his superfluous energy, he leapt back again on Isabel's lap, with his tongue quivering in his open mouth – his tail wagging softly, and his eye on Miss Pink, inquiring how she liked a dog in her drawing-room!

'I hope my dog has not disturbed you, ma'am?' said Lady Lydiard, advancing from the mat at the doorway, on which she had patiently waited until the raptures of Tommie subsided into repose.

Miss Pink, trembling between terror and indignation, acknowledged Lady Lydiard's polite inquiry by a ceremonious bow, and an answer which administered by implication a dignified reproof. 'Your Ladyship's dog does not appear to be a very well-trained animal,' the ex-schoolmistress remarked.

'Well trained?' Lady Lydiard repeated, as if the expression was perfectly unintelligible to her. 'I don't think you have had much experience of dogs, ma'am.' She turned to Isabel, and embraced her tenderly. 'Give me a kiss, my dear – you don't know how wretched I have been since you left me.' She looked back again at Miss Pink. 'You are not, perhaps, aware, ma'am, that my dog is devotedly attached to your niece. A dog's love has been considered by many great men (whose names at the moment escape me) as the most touching and disinterested of all earthly affections.' She looked the other way, and discovered the lawyer. 'How do you do, Mr Troy? It's a pleasant surprise to find you here. The house was so dull without Isabel that I really couldn't put off seeing her any longer. When you are more used to Tommie, Miss Pink, you will understand and admire him. *You* understand and admire him, Isabel – don't you? My child! you are not looking well. I shall take you back with me, when the horses have had their rest. We shall never be happy away from each other.'

Having expressed her sentiments, distributed her greetings, and defended her dog – all, as it were, in one breath – Lady Lydiard sat down by Isabel's side, and opened a large green fan that hung at her girdle. 'You have no idea, Miss Pink, how fat people suffer in hot weather,' said the old lady, using her fan vigorously.

Miss Pink's eyes dropped modestly to the ground – 'fat' was such a coarse word to use, if a lady *must* speak of her own superfluous flesh! 'May I offer some refreshment?' Miss Pink asked, mincingly. 'A cup of tea?'

Lady Lydiard shook her head.

'A glass of water?'

Lady Lydiard declined this last hospitable proposal with an exclamation of disgust. 'Have you got any beer?' she inquired.

'I beg your Ladyship's pardon,' said Miss Pink, doubting the evidence of her own ears. 'Did you say – beer?'

Lady Lydiard gesticulated vehemently with her fan. 'Yes, to be sure! Beer! beer!'

Miss Pink rose, with a countenance expressive of genteel

disgust, and rang the bell. 'I think you have beer down stairs, Susan?' she said, when the maid appeared at the door.

'Yes, Miss.'

'A glass of beer for Lady Lydiard,' said Miss Pink – under protest.

'Bring it in a jug,' shouted her Ladyship, as the maid left the room. 'I like to froth it up for myself,' she continued, addressing Miss Pink. 'Isabel sometimes does it for me, when she is at home – don't you, my dear?'

Miss Pink had been waiting her opportunity to assert her own claim to the possession of her own niece, from the time when Lady Lydiard had coolly declared her intention of taking Isabel back with her. The opportunity now presented itself.

'Your Ladyship will pardon me,' she said, 'if I remark that my niece's home is under my humble roof. I am properly sensible, I hope, of your kindness to Isabel; but while she remains the object of a disgraceful suspicion she remains with me.'

Lady Lydiard closed her fan with an angry snap.

'You are completely mistaken, Miss Pink. You may not mean it – but you speak most unjustly if you say that your niece is an object of suspicion to me, or to anybody in my house.'

Mr Troy, quietly listening up to this point, now interposed to stop the discussion before it could degenerate into a personal quarrel. His keen observation, aided by his accurate knowledge of his client's character, had plainly revealed to him what was passing in Lady Lydiard's mind. She had entered the house, feeling (perhaps unconsciously) a jealousy of Miss Pink, as her predecessor in Isabel's affections, and as the natural protectress of the girl under existing circumstances. Miss Pink's reception of her dog had additionally irritated the old lady. She had taken a malicious pleasure in shocking the schoolmistress's sense of propriety – and she was now only too ready to proceed to further extremities on the delicate question of Isabel's justification for leaving her house. For Isabel's own sake, therefore – to say nothing of other reasons – it was urgently desirable to keep the peace between the two ladies. With this excellent object in view, Mr Troy seized his opportunity of striking into the conversation for the first time.

'Pardon me, Lady Lydiard,' he said, 'you are speaking of a subject which has been already sufficiently discussed between

Miss Pink and myself. I think we shall do better not to dwell uselessly on past events, but to direct our attention to the future. We are all equally satisfied of the complete rectitude of Miss Isabel's conduct, and we are all equally interested in the vindication of her good name.'

Whether these temperate words would of themselves have exercised the pacifying influence at which Mr Troy aimed may be doubtful. But, as he ceased speaking, a powerful auxiliary appeared in the shape of the beer. Lady Lydiard seized on the jug, and filled the tumbler for herself with an unsteady hand. Miss Pink, trembling for the integrity of her carpet, and scandalized at seeing a peeress drinking beer like a washerwoman, forgot the sharp answer that was just rising to her lips when the lawyer interfered. 'Small!' said Lady Lydiard, setting down the empty tumbler, and referring to the quality of the beer. 'But very pleasant and refreshing. What's the servant's name? Susan? Well, Susan, I was dying of thirst; and you have saved my life. You can leave the jug – I dare say I shall empty it before I go.'

Mr Troy, watching Miss Pink's face, saw that it was time to change the subject again.

'Did you notice the old village, Lady Lydiard, on your way here?' he asked. 'The artists consider it one of the most picturesque places in England.'

'I noticed that it was a very dirty village,' Lady Lydiard answered, still bent on making herself disagreeable to Miss Pink. 'The artists may say what they please; I see nothing to admire in rotten cottages, and bad drainage, and ignorant people. I suppose the neighbourhood has its advantages. It looks dull enough, to my mind.'

Isabel had hitherto modestly restricted her exertions to keeping Tommie quiet on her lap. Like Mr Troy, she occasionally looked at her aunt – and she now made a timid attempt to defend the neighbourhood, as a duty that she owed to Miss Pink.

'Oh, my Lady! don't say it's a dull neighbourhood,' she pleaded. 'There are such pretty walks all round us. And, when you get to the hills, the view is beautiful.'

Lady Lydiard's answer to this was a little masterpiece of good-humoured contempt. She patted Isabel's cheek, and said, 'Pooh! pooh!'

'Your Ladyship does not admire the beauties of Nature,' Miss Pink remarked, with a compassionate smile. 'As we get older, no doubt our sight begins to fail —— '

'And we leave off canting about the beauties of Nature,' added Lady Lydiard. 'I hate the country. Give me London, and the pleasures of society.'

'Come! come! Do the country justice, Lady Lydiard!' put in peace-making Mr Troy. 'There is plenty of society to be found out of London – as good society as the world can show.'

'The sort of society,' added Miss Pink, 'which is to be found, for example, in this neighbourhood. Her Ladyship is evidently not aware that persons of distinction surround us, whichever way we turn. I may instance among others, the Honourable Mr Hardyman —— '

Lady Lydiard, in the act of pouring out a second glassful of beer, suddenly set down the jug.

'Who is that you're talking of, Miss Pink?'

'I am talking of our neighbour, Lady Lydiard – the Honourable Mr Hardyman.'

'Do you mean Alfred Hardyman – the man who breeds the horses?'

'The distinguished gentleman who owns the famous stud-farm,' said Miss Pink, correcting the bluntly-direct form in which Lady Lydiard had put her question.

'Is he in the habit of visiting here?' the old lady inquired, with a sudden appearance of anxiety. 'Do you know him?'

'I had the honour of being introduced to Mr Hardyman at our last flower show,' Miss Pink replied. 'He has not yet favoured me with a visit.'

Lady Lydiard's anxiety appeared to be to some extent relieved.

'I knew that Hardyman's farm was in this county,' she said; 'but I had no notion that it was in the neighbourhood of South Morden. How far away is he – ten or a dozen miles, eh?'

'Not more than three miles,' answered Miss Pink. 'We consider him quite a near neighbour of ours.'

Renewed anxiety showed itself in Lady Lydiard. She looked round sharply at Isabel. The girl's head was bent so low over the rough head of the dog that her face was almost entirely concealed from view. So far as appearances went, she seemed to be entirely absorbed in fondling Tommie. Lady Lydiard roused her with a tap of the green fan.

'Take Tommie out, Isabel, for a run in the garden,' she said. 'He won't sit still much longer – and he may annoy Miss Pink. Mr Troy, will you kindly help Isabel to keep my ill-trained dog in order?'

Mr Troy got on his feet, and, not very willingly, followed Isabel out of the room. 'They will quarrel now, to a dead certainty!' he thought to himself, as he closed the door. 'Have you any idea of what this means?' he said to his companion, as he joined her in the hall. 'What has Mr Hardyman done to excite all this interest in him?'

Isabel's guilty colour rose. She knew perfectly well that Hardyman's unconcealed admiration of her was the guiding motive of Lady Lydiard's inquiries. If she had told the truth, Mr Troy would have unquestionably returned to the drawing-room, with or without an acceptable excuse for intruding himself. But Isabel was a woman; and her answer, it is needless to say, was 'I don't know, I'm sure.'

In the mean time, the interview between the two ladies began in a manner which would have astonished Mr Troy – they were both silent. For once in her life Lady Lydiard was considering what she should say, before she said it. Miss Pink, on her side, naturally waited to hear what object her Ladyship had in view – waited, until her small reserve of patience gave way. Urged by irresistible curiosity, she spoke first.

'Have you anything to say to me in private?' she asked.

Lady Lydiard had not got to the end of her reflections. She said 'Yes!' – and she said no more.

'Is it anything relating to my niece?' persisted Miss Pink.

Still immersed in her reflections, Lady Lydiard suddenly rose to the surface, and spoke her mind, as usual.

'About your niece, ma'am. The other day Mr Hardyman called at my house, and saw Isabel.'

'Yes,' said Miss Pink, politely attentive, but not in the least interested, so far.

'That's not all, ma'am. Mr Hardyman admires Isabel; he owned it to me himself in so many words.'

Miss Pink listened, with a courteous inclination of her head. She looked mildly gratified, nothing more. Lady Lydiard proceeded:

'You and I think differently on many matters,' she said. 'But we are both agreed, I am sure, in feeling the sincerest interest in Isabel's welfare. I beg to suggest to you, Miss Pink, that Mr Hardyman, as a near neighbour of yours, is a very undesirable neighbour while Isabel remains in your house.'

Saying those words, under a strong conviction of the serious importance of the subject, Lady Lydiard insensibly recovered the manner and resumed the language which befitted a lady of her rank. Miss Pink, noticing the change, set it down to an expression of pride on the part of her visitor which, in referring to Isabel, assailed indirectly the social position of Isabel's aunt.

'I fail entirely to understand what your Ladyship means,' she said coldly.

Lady Lydiard, on her side, looked in undisguised amazement at Miss Pink.

'Haven't I told you already that Mr Hardyman admires your niece?' she asked.

'Naturally,' said Miss Pink. 'Isabel inherits her lamented mother's personal advantages. If Mr Hardyman admires her, Mr Hardyman shows his good taste.'

Lady Lydiard's eyes opened wider and wider in wonder. 'My good lady!' she exclaimed, 'is it possible you don't know that when a man admires a women he doesn't stop there? He falls in love with her (as the saying is) next.'

'So I have heard,' said Miss Pink.

'So you have *heard*?' repeated Lady Lydiard. 'If Mr Hardyman finds his way to Isabel I can tell you what you will *see*. Catch the two together, ma'am – and you will see Mr Hardyman making love to your niece.'

'Under due restrictions, Lady Lydiard, and with my permission first obtained, of course, I see no objection to Mr Hardyman paying his addresses to Isabel.'

'The woman is mad!' cried Lady Lydiard. 'Do you actually suppose, Miss Pink, that Alfred Hardyman could, by any earthly possibility, marry your niece!'

Not even Miss Pink's politeness could submit to such a question as this. She rose indignantly from her chair. 'Are you aware, Lady Lydiard, that the doubt you have just expressed is an insult to my niece, and an insult to Me?'

'Are *you* aware of who Mr Hardyman really is?' retorted her Ladyship. 'Or do you judge of his position by the vocation in life which he has perversely chosen to adopt? I can tell you, if you do, that Alfred Hardyman is the younger son of one of the oldest barons in the English Peerage, and that his mother is related by marriage to the Royal family of Wurtemberg.'

Miss Pink received the full shock of this information without receding from her position by a hair's breadth.

'An English gentlewoman offers a fit alliance to any man living who seeks her hand in marriage,' said Miss Pink. 'Isabel's mother (you may not be aware of it) was the daughter of an English clergyman —— '

'And Isabel's father was a chemist in a country town,' added Lady Lydiard.

'Isabel's father,' rejoined Miss Pink, 'was attached in a most responsible capacity to the useful and honourable profession of Medicine. Isabel is, in the strictest sense of the word, a young gentlewoman. If you contradict that for a single instant, Lady Lydiard, you will oblige me to leave the room.'

Those last words produced a result which Miss Pink had not anticipated – they roused Lady Lydiard to assert herself. As usual in such cases, she rose superior to her own eccentricity. Confronting Miss Pink, she now spoke and looked with the gracious courtesy and the unpresuming self-confidence of the order to which she belonged.

'For Isabel's own sake, and for the quieting of my conscience,' she answered, 'I will say one word more, Miss Pink, before I relieve you of my presence. Considering my age and my opportunities, I may claim to know quite as much as you do of the laws and customs which regulate society in our time. Without contesting your niece's social position – and without the slightest intention of insulting you – I repeat that the rank which Mr Hardyman inherits makes it simply impossible for him even to think of marrying Isabel. You will do well not to give him any opportunities of meeting with her alone. And you will do better still (seeing that he is so near a neighbour of yours) if you permit Isabel to return to my protection, for a time at least. I will wait to hear from you when you have thought the matter over at your leisure. In the mean time, if I have inadvertently offended you, I ask your pardon – and I wish you good evening.'

She bowed, and walked to the door. Miss Pink, as resolute as ever in maintaining her pretensions, made an effort to match the great lady on her own ground.

'Before you go, Lady Lydiard, I beg to apologize if I have spoken too warmly on my side,' she said. 'Permit me to send for your carriage.'

'Thank you, Miss Pink. My carriage is only at the village inn. I shall enjoy a little walk in the cool evening air. Mr Troy, I have no doubt, will give me his arm.' She bowed once more, and quietly left the room.

Reaching the little back garden of the villa, through an open door at the farther end of the hall, Lady Lydiard found Tommie rolling luxuriously on Miss Pink's flower-beds, and Isabel and Mr Troy in close consultation on the gravel walk. She spoke to the lawyer first.

'They are baiting the horses at the inn,' she said. 'I want your arm, Mr Troy, as far as the village – and, in return, I will take you back to London with me. I have to ask your advice about one or two little matters, and this is a good opportunity.'

'With the greatest pleasure, Lady Lydiard. I suppose I must say good-bye to Miss Pink?'

'A word of advice to you, Mr Troy. Take care how you ruffle Miss Pink's sense of her own importance. Another word for your private ear. Miss Pink is a fool.'

On the lawyer's withdrawal, Lady Lydiard put her arm fondly round Isabel's waist. 'What were you and Mr Troy so busy in talking about?' she asked.

'We were talking, my Lady, about tracing the person who stole the money,' Isabel answered, rather sadly. 'It seems a far more difficult matter than I supposed it to be. I try not to lose patience and hope – but it is a little hard to feel that appearances are against me, and to wait day after day in vain for the discovery that is to set me right.'

'You are a dear good child,' said Lady Lydiard; 'and you are more precious to me than ever. Don't despair, Isabel. With Mr Troy's means of inquiring, and with my means of paying, the discovery of the thief cannot be much longer delayed. If you don't return to me soon, I shall come back and see you again. Your aunt hates the sight of me – but I don't care two straws for that,' remarked Lady Lydiard, showing the undignified side of her character once more. 'Listen to me, Isabel! I have no wish to lower your aunt in your estimation, but I feel far more confidence in your good sense than in hers. Mr Hardyman's business has taken him to France for the present. It is at least possible that you may meet with him on his return. If you do, keep him at a distance, my dear – politely, of course. There! there! you needn't turn red; I am not blaming you; I am only giving you a little good advice. In your position you cannot possibly be too careful. Here is Mr Troy! You must come to the gate with us, Isabel, or we shall never get Tommie away from you; I am only his second favourite; you have the first place in his affections. God bless and prosper you, my child! – I wish to Heaven you were going back to London with me! Well, Mr Troy, how have you done with Miss Pink? Have you offended that terrible "gentlewoman" (hateful word!); or has it been all the other way, and has she given you a kiss at parting?'

Mr Troy smiled mysteriously, and changed the subject. His brief parting interview with the lady of the house was not of a nature to be rashly related. Miss Pink had not only positively assured him that her visitor was the most ill-bred woman she had ever met with, but had further accused Lady Lydiard of shaking her confidence in the aristocracy of her native country. 'For the first time in my life,' said Miss Pink, 'I feel that something is to be said for the Republican point of view; and I am not indisposed to admit that the constitution of the United States *has* its advantages!'

CHAPTER XII

The conference between Lady Lydiard and Mr Troy, on the way back to London, led to some practical results.

Hearing from her legal adviser that the inquiry after the missing money was for a moment at a standstill, Lady Lydiard made one of those bold suggestions with which she was accustomed to startle her friends in cases of emergency. She had heard favourable reports of the extraordinary ingenuity of the French police; and she now proposed sending to Paris for assistance, after first consulting her nephew, Mr Felix Sweetsir. 'Felix knows Paris as well as he knows London,' she remarked. 'He is an idle man, and it is quite likely that he will relieve us of all trouble by taking the matter into his own hands. In any case, he is sure to know who are the right people to address in our present necessity. What do you say?'

Mr Troy, in reply, expressed his doubts as to the wisdom of employing foreigners in a delicate investigation which required an accurate knowledge of English customs and English character. Waiving this objection, he approved of the idea of consulting her Ladyship's nephew. 'Mr Sweetsir is a man of the world,' he said. 'In putting the case before him, we are sure to have it presented to us from a new point of view.' Acting on this favourable expression of opinion, Lady Lydiard wrote to her nephew. On the day after the visit to Miss Pink, the proposed council of three was held at Lady Lydiard's house.

Felix, never punctual at keeping an appointment, was even later than usual on this occasion. He made his apologies with his hand pressed upon his forehead, and his voice expressive of the languor and discouragement of a suffering man.

'The beastly English climate is telling on my nerves,' said Mr Sweetsir – 'the horrid weight of the atmosphere, after the exhilarating air of Paris; the intolerable dirt and dullness of London, you know. I was in bed, my dear aunt, when I received your letter. You may imagine the completely demoralised state I was in, when I tell you of the effect which the news of the robbery produced on me. I fell back on my pillow, as if I had been shot. Your Ladyship should really be a little more careful in communicating these disagreeable surprises to a sensitively-organised man. Never mind – my valet is a perfect treasure; he brought me some drops of ether on a lump of sugar. I said, "Alfred" (his name is Alfred), "put me into my clothes!" Alfred put me in. I assure you it reminded me of my young days, when I was put into my first pair of trousers. Has Alfred forgotten anything? Have I got my braces on? Have I come out in my shirt-sleeves? Well, dear aunt; – well, Mr Troy! – what can I say? What can I do?'

Lady Lydiard, entirely without sympathy for nervous suffering, nodded to the lawyer. 'You tell him,' she said.

'I believe I speak for her Ladyship,' Mr Troy began, 'when I say that we should like to hear, in the first place, how the whole case strikes you, Mr Sweetsir?'

'Tell it me all over again,' said Felix.

Patient Mr Troy told it all over again – and waited for the result.

'Well?' said Felix.

'Well?' said Mr Troy. 'Where does the suspicion of robbery rest in your opinion? You look at the theft of the bank-note with a fresh eye.'

'You mentioned a clergyman just now,' said Felix. 'The man, you know, to whom the money was sent. What was his name?'

'The Reverend Samuel Bradstock.'

'You want me to name the person whom I suspect?'

'Yes, if you please,' said Mr Troy.

'I suspect the Reverend Samuel Bradstock,' said Felix.

'If you have come here to make stupid jokes,' interposed Lady Lydiard, 'you had better go back to your bed again. We want a serious opinion.'

'You *have* a serious opinion,' Felix coolly rejoined. 'I never was more in earnest in my life. Your Ladyship is not aware of the first principle to be adopted in cases of suspicion. One proceeds on what I will call the exhaustive system of reasoning. Thus: – Does suspicion point to the honest servants down stairs? No. To your Ladyship's adopted daughter? Appearances are against the poor girl; but you know her better than to trust to appearances. Are you suspicious of Moody? No. Of Hardyman – who was in the house at the time? Ridiculous! But I was in the house at the time, too. Do you suspect Me? Just so! That idea is ridiculous, too. Now let us sum up. Servants, adopted daughter, Moody, Hardyman, Sweetsir – all beyond suspicion. Who is left? The Reverend Samuel Bradstock.'

This ingenious exposition of 'the exhaustive system of reasoning', failed to produce any effect on Lady Lydiard. 'You are wasting our time,' she said sharply. 'You know as well as I do that you are talking nonsense.'

'I don't,' said Felix. 'Taking the gentlemanly professions all round, I know of no men who are so eager to get money, and who have so few scruples about how they get it, as the parsons. Where is there a man in any other profession who perpetually worries you for money? – who holds the bag under your nose for money? – who sends his clerk round from door to door to beg a few shillings of you, and calls it an "Easter offering"? The parson does all this. Bradstock is a parson. I put it logically. Bowl me over, if you can.'

Mr Troy attempted to 'bowl him over', nevertheless. Lady Lydiard wisely interposed.

'When a man persists in talking nonsense,' she said, 'silence is the best answer; anything else only encourages him.' She turned to Felix. 'I have a question to ask you,' she went on. 'You will either give me a serious reply, or wish me good morning.' With this brief preface, she made her inquiry as to the wisdom and possibility of engaging the services of the French police.

Felix took exactly the view of the matter which had been already expressed by Mr Troy. 'Superior in intelligence,' he said, 'but not superior in courage, to the English police. Capable of performing wonders on their own ground and among their own people. But, my dear aunt, the two most dissimilar nations on the face of the earth are the English and the French. The French police may speak our language – but they are incapable of understanding our national character and our national manners. Set them to work on a private inquiry in the city of Pekin – and they would get on in time with the Chinese people. Set them to work in the city of London – and the English people would remain, from first to last, the same impenetrable mystery to them. In my belief the London Sunday would be enough of itself to drive them back to Paris in despair. No balls, no concerts, no theatres, not even a museum or a picture-gallery open; every shop shut up but the gin-shop; and nothing moving but the church bells and the men who sell the penny ices. Hundreds of Frenchmen come to see me on their first arrival in England. Every man of them rushes back to Paris on the second Saturday of his visit; rather than confront the horrors of a second Sunday in London! However, you can try it if you like. Send me a written abstract of the case, and I will forward it to one of the official people in the Rue Jerusalem, who will do anything he can to oblige me. Of course,' said Felix, turning to Mr Troy, 'some of you have got the number of the lost bank-note? If the thief has tried to pass it in Paris, my man may be of some use to you.'

'Three of us have got the number of the note,' answered Mr Troy; 'Miss Isabel Miller, Mr Moody, and myself.'

'Very good,' said Felix. 'Send me the number, with the abstract of the case. Is there anything else I can do towards recovering the money?' he asked, turning to his aunt. 'There is one lucky circumstance in connection with this loss – isn't there? It has fallen on a person who is rich enough to take it easy. Good Heavens! suppose it had been *my* loss!'

'It has fallen doubly on me,' said Lady Lydiard; 'and I am certainly not rich enough to take it *that* easy. The money was destined to a charitable purpose; and I have felt it my duty to pay it again.'

Felix rose and approached his aunt's chair with faltering steps, as became a suffering man. He took Lady Lydiard's hand and kissed it with enthusiastic admiration.

'You excellent creature!' he said. 'You may not think it, but you reconcile me to human nature. How generous! how noble! I think I'll go to bed again, Mr Troy, if you really don't want any more of me. My head feels giddy and my legs tremble under me. It doesn't matter; I shall feel easier when Alfred has taken me out of my clothes again. God bless you, my dear aunt! I never felt so proud of being related to you as I do to-day. Good-morning Mr Troy! Don't forget the abstract of the case; and don't trouble yourself to see me to the door. I dare say I shan't tumble down stairs; and, if I do, there's the porter in the hall to pick me up again. Enviable porter! as fat as butter and as idle as a pig! *Au revoir! au revoir!*' He kissed his hand, and drifted feebly out of the room. Sweetsir, one might say, in a state of eclipse; but still the serviceable Sweetsir, who was never consulted in vain by the fortunate people privileged to call him friend!

'Is he really ill, do you think?' Mr Troy asked.

'My nephew has turned fifty,' Lady Lydiard answered, 'and he persists in living as if he was a young man. Every now and then Nature says to him, "Felix you are old!" And Felix goes to bed, and says it's his nerves.'

'I suppose he is to be trusted to keep his word about writing to Paris?' pursued the lawyer.

'Oh, yes! He may delay doing it; but he will do it. In spite of his lackadaisical manner, he has moments of energy that would surprise you. Talking of surprises, I have something to tell you about Moody. Within the last day or two there has been a marked change in him – a change for the worse.'

'You astonish me, Lady Lydiard! In what way has Moody deteriorated?'

'You shall hear. Yesterday was Friday. You took him out with you, on business, early in the morning.'

Mr Troy bowed, and said nothing. He had not thought it desirable to mention the interview at which Old Sharon had cheated him of his guinea.

'In the course of the afternoon,' pursued Lady Lydiard, 'I happened to want him, and I was informed that Moody had gone out again. Where had he gone? Nobody knew. Had he left word when he would be back? He had left no message of any sort. Of course, he is not in the position of an ordinary servant. I don't expect him to ask permission to go out. But I do expect him to leave word downstairs of the time at which he is likely to return. When he did come back, after an absence of some hours, I naturally asked for an explanation. Would you believe it? he simply informed me that he had been away on business of his own; expressed no regret, and offered no explanation – in short, spoke as if he was an independent gentleman. You may not think it, but I kept my temper. I merely remarked that I hoped it would not happen again. He made me a bow, and he said, "My business is not completed yet, my Lady. I cannot guarantee that it may not call me away again at a moment's notice." What do you think of that? Nine people out of ten would have given him warning to leave their service. I begin to think I am a wonderful woman – I only pointed to the door. One does hear sometimes of men's brains softening in the most unexpected manner. I have my suspicions of Moody's brains, I can tell you.'

Mr Troy's suspicions took a different direction: they pointed along the line of streets which led to Old Sharon's lodgings. Discreetly silent as to the turn which his thoughts had taken, he merely expressed himself as feeling too much surprised to offer any opinion at all.

'Wait a little,' said Lady Lydiard, 'I haven't done surprising you yet. You have seen a boy here in a page's livery, I think? Well, he is a good boy; and he has gone home for a week's holiday with his friends. The proper person to supply his place with the boots and shoes and other small employments, is of course the youngest footman, a lad only a few years older than himself. What do you think Moody does? Engages a stranger, with the house full of idle men-servants already, to fill the page's place. At intervals this morning I heard them wonder-fully merry in the servant's hall – *so* merry that the noise and laughter found its way up stairs to the breakfast-room. I like my servants to be in good spirits; but it certainly did strike me that they were getting beyond reasonable limits. I questioned my maid, and was informed that the noise was all due to the jokes of the strangest old man that ever was seen. In other words, to the person whom my steward had taken it on himself to engage in the page's absence. I spoke to Moody on the subject. He answered in an odd, confused way, that he had exercised his discretion to the best of his judgment, and that (if I wished it), he would tell the old man to keep his good spirits under better control. I asked him how he came to hear of the man. He only answered, "By accident, my Lady" – and not one more word could I get out of him, good or bad. Moody engages the servants, as you know; but on every other occasion he has invariably consulted me before an engagement was settled. I really don't feel at all sure about this person who has been so strangely introduced into the house – he may be a drunkard or a thief. I wish you would speak to Moody yourself, Mr Troy. Do you mind ringing the bell?'

Mr Troy rose, as a matter of course, and rang the bell.

He was by this time, it is needless to say, convinced that Moody had not only gone back to consult Old Sharon on his own responsibility, but, worse still, had taken the un-warrantable liberty of introducing him, as a spy, into the house. To communicate this explanation to Lady Lydiard would, in her present humour, be simply to produce the dismissal of the steward from her service. The only other alternative was to ask leave to interrogate Moody privately, and, after duly reproving him, to insist on the departure of Old Sharon as the one condition on which Mr Troy would consent to keep Lady Lydiard in ignorance of the truth.

'I think I shall manage better with Moody, if your Ladyship will permit me to see him in private,' the lawyer said. 'Shall I go downstairs and speak with him in his own room?'

'Why should you trouble yourself to do that?' said her Ladyship. 'See him here; and I will go into the boudoir.'

As she made that reply the footman appeared at the drawing-room door.

'Send Moody here,' said Lady Lydiard.

The footman's answer, delivered at that moment, assumed an importance which was not expressed in the footman's words. 'My Lady,' he said, 'Mr Moody has gone out.'

CHAPTER XIII

While the strange proceedings of the steward were the subject of conversation between Lady Lydiard and Mr Troy, Moody was alone in his room, occupied in writing to Isabel. Being unwilling that any eyes but his own should see the address, he had himself posted his letter; the time that he had chosen for leaving the house proving, unfortunately, to be also the time proposed by her Ladyship for his interview with the lawyer. In ten minutes after the footman had reported his absence, Moody returned. It was then too late to present himself in the drawing-room. In the interval, Mr Troy had taken his leave, and Moody's position had dropped a degree lower in Lady Lydiard's estimation.

Isabel received her letter by the next morning's post. If any justification of Mr Troy's suspicions had been needed, the terms in which Moody wrote would have amply supplied it.

"Dear Isabel" (I hope I may call you 'Isabel' without offending you, in your present trouble?) – I have a proposal to make, which, whether you accept it or not, I beg you will keep a secret from every living creature but ourselves. You will understand my request, when I add that these lines relate to the matter of tracing the stolen bank-note.

'I have been privately in communication with a person in London, who is, as I believe, the one person competent to help us in gaining our end. He has already made many inquiries in private. With some of them I am acquainted; the rest he has thus far kept to himself. The person to whom I allude, particularly wishes to have half an hour's conversation with you – in my presence. I am bound to warn you that he is a very strange and very ugly old man; and I can only hope that you will look over his personal appearance in consideration of what he is likely to do for your future advantage.

'Can you conveniently meet us, at the farther end of the row of villas in which your aunt lives, the day after to-morrow, at four o'clock? Let me have a line to say if you will keep the appointment, and if the hour named will suit you. And believe me your devoted friend and servant,

'ROBERT MOODY.'

The lawyer's warning to her to be careful how she yielded too readily to any proposal of Moody's recurred to Isabel's mind while she read those lines. Being pledged to secrecy, she could not consult Mr Troy – she was left to decide for herself.

No obstacle stood in the way of her free choice of alternatives. After their early dinner at three o'clock, Miss Pink habitually retired to her own room 'to meditate', as she expressed it. Her 'meditations' inevitably ended in a sound sleep of some hours; and during that interval Isabel was at liberty to do as she pleased. After considerable hesitation, her implicit belief in Moody's truth and devotion, assisted by a strong feeling of curiosity to see the companion with whom the steward had associated himself, decided Isabel on consenting to keep the appointment.

Taking up her position beyond the houses, on the day and at the hour mentioned by Moody, she believed herself to be fully prepared for the most unfavourable impression which the most disagreeable of all possible strangers could produce.

But the first appearance of Old Sharon – as dirty as ever, clothed in a long, frowsy, grey overcoat, with his pug-dog at his heels, and his smoke-blackened pipe in his mouth; with a tall white hat on his head, which looked as if it had been picked up in a gutter, a hideous leer in his eyes, and a jaunty trip in his walk – took her so completely by surprise that she could only return Moody's friendly greeting by silently pressing his hand. As for Moody's companion, to look at him for a second time was more than she had resolution to do. She kept her eyes fixed on the pug-dog, and with good reason: as far as appearances went, he was indisputably the nobler animal of the two.

Under the circumstances, the interview threatened to begin in a very embarrassing manner. Moody, disheartened by Isabel's silence, made no attempt to set the conversation going; he looked as if he meditated a hasty retreat to the railway station which he had just left. Fortunately, he had at his side the right man (for once) in the right place. Old Sharon's effrontery was equal to any emergency.

'I am not a nice-looking old man, my dear, am I?' he said, leering at Isabel with cunning, half-closed eyes. 'Bless your heart! you'll soon get used to me! You see, I am the sort of colour, as they say at the linen-drapers', that doesn't wash well. It's all through love; upon my life it is! Early in the present century I had my young affections blighted; and I've neglected myself ever since. Disappointment takes different forms, Miss, in different men. I don't think I have had heart enough to brush my hair for the last fifty years. She was a magnificent woman, Mr Moody, and she dropped me like a hot potato. Dreadful! dreadful! Let us pursue this painful subject no further. Ha! here's a pretty country! Here's a nice blue sky! I admire the country, Miss; I see so little of it, you know. Have you any objection to walk along into the fields? The fields, my dear, bring out all the poetry of my nature. Where's the dog? Here, Puggy! Puggy! hunt about, my man, and find some dog-grass. Does his inside good, you know, after a meat diet in London. Lord! how I feel my spirits rising in this fine air! Does my complexion look any brighter, Miss? Will you run a race with me, Mr Moody, or will you oblige me with a back at leap-frog? I'm not mad, my dear young lady; I'm only merry. I live, you see, in the London stink; and the smell of the hedges and the wild flowers is too much for me at first. It gets into my head, it does. I'm drunk! As I live by bread, I'm drunk on fresh air! Oh! what a jolly day! Oh!

how young and innocent I do feel!' Here his innocence got the better of him, and he began to sing, 'I wish I were a little fly, in my love's bosom for to lie!' 'Hullo! here we are on the nice soft grass! and, oh, my gracious! there's a bank running down into a hollow! I can't stand that, you know. Mr Moody, hold my hat, and take the greatest care of it. Here goes for a roll down the bank!'

He handed his horrible hat to the astonished Moody, laid himself flat on the top of the bank, and deliberately rolled down it, exactly as he might have done when he was a boy. The tails of his long grey coat flew madly in the wind: the dog pursued him, jumping over him, and barking with delight; he shouted and screamed in answer to the dog, as he rolled over and over faster and faster; and, when he got up, on the level ground, and called out cheerfully to his companions standing above him, 'I say, you two, I feel twenty years younger already!' – human gravity could hold out no longer. The sad and silent Moody smiled, and Isabel burst into fits of laughter.

'There,' he said, 'didn't I tell you you would get used to me, Miss? There's a deal of life left in the old man yet – isn't there? Shy me down, my hat, Mr Moody. And now we'll get to business!' He turned round to the dog still barking at his heels. 'Business, Puggy!' he called out sharply, and Puggy instantly shut up his mouth, and said no more.

'Well, now,' Old Sharon resumed when he had joined his friends and had got his breath again, 'let's have a little talk about yourself, Miss. Has Mr Moody told you who I am, and what I want with you? Very good. May I offer you my arm? No! You like to be independent, don't you? All right – I don't object. I am an amiable old man, I am. About this Lady Lydiard, now? Suppose you tell me how you first got acquainted with her?'

In some surprise at this question, Isabel told her little story. Observing Sharon's face while she was speaking, Moody saw that he was not paying the smallest attention to the narrative. His sharp shameless black eyes watched the girl's face absently; his gross lips curled upwards in a sardonic and self-satisfied smile. He was evidently setting a trap for her of some kind. Without a word of warning – while Isabel was in the middle of a sentence – the trap opened, with the opening of Old Sharon's lips.

'I say,' he burst out. 'How came *you* to seal her Ladyship's letter – eh?'

The question bore no sort of relation, direct or indirect, to what Isabel happened to be saying at the moment. In the sudden surprise of hearing it, she started and fixed her eyes in astonishment on Sharon's face. The old vagabond chuckled to himself. 'Did you see that?' he whispered to Moody. 'I beg your pardon, Miss,' he went on; 'I won't interrupt you again. Lord! how interesting it is! – ain't it, Mr Moody? Please to go on, Miss.'

But Isabel, though she spoke with perfect sweetness and temper, declined to go on. 'I had better tell you, sir, how I came to seal her Ladyship's letter,' she said. 'If I may venture on giving my opinion, *that* part of my story seems to be the only part of it which relates to your business with me to-day.'

Without further preface she described the circumstances which had led to her assuming the perilous responsibility of sealing the letter. Old Sharon's wandering attention began to wander again: he was evidently occupied in setting another trap. For the second time he interrupted Isabel in the middle of a sentence. Suddenly stopping short, he pointed to some sheep, at the farther end of the field through which they happened to be passing at the moment.

'There's a pretty sight,' he said. 'There are the innocent sheep a-feeding – all following each other as usual. And there's the sly dog waiting behind the gate till the sheep wants his services. Reminds me of Old Sharon and the public!' He chuckled over the discovery of the remarkable similarity between the sheep-dog and himself, and the sheep and the public – and then burst upon Isabel with a second question. 'I say! didn't you look at the letter before you sealed it?'

'Certainly not!' Isabel answered.

'Not even at the address?'

'No!'

'Thinking of something else – eh?'

'Very likely,' said Isabel.

'Was it your new bonnet, my dear?'

Isabel laughed. 'Women are not always thinking of their new bonnets,' she answered.

Old Sharon, to all appearance, dropped the subject there.

He lifted his lean brown forefinger and pointed again – this time to a house at a short distance from them. 'That's a farm-house, surely?' he said. 'I'm thirsty, after my roll down the hill. Do you think, Miss, they would give me a drink of milk?'

'I am sure they would,' said Isabel. 'I know the people. Shall I go and ask them?'

'Thank you, my dear. One word more before you go. About the sealing of that letter? What *could* you have been thinking of while you were doing it?' He looked hard at her, and took her suddenly by the arm. 'Was it your sweetheart?' he asked, in a whisper.

The question instantly reminded Isabel that she had been thinking of Hardyman while she sealed the letter. She blushed as the remembrance crossed her mind. Robert, noticing the embarrassment, spoke sharply to Old Sharon. 'You have no right to put such a question to a young lady,' he said. 'Be a little more careful for the future.'

'There! there! don't be hard on me,' pleaded the old rogue. 'An ugly old man like me may make his innocent little joke – eh, Miss? I'm sure you're too sweet-tempered to be angry when I meant no offence. Show me that you bear no malice. Go, like a forgiving young angel, and ask for the milk.'

Nobody appealed to Isabel's sweetness of temper in vain. 'I will do it with pleasure,' she said – and hastened away to the farm-house.

CHAPTER XIV

The instant Isabel was out of hearing, Old Sharon slapped Moody on the shoulder to rouse his attention. 'I've got her out of the way,' he said, 'now listen to me. My business with the young angel is done – I may go back to London.'

Moody looked at him with astonishment.

'Lord! how little you know of thieves!' exclaimed Old Sharon. 'Why, man alive, I have tried her with two plain tests!

If you wanted a proof of her innocence, there it was, as plain as the nose in your face. Did you hear me ask her how she came to seal the letter – just when her mind was running on something else?'

'I heard you,' said Moody.

'Did you see how she started and stared at me?'

'I did.'

'Well, I can tell you this – if she *had* stolen the money she would neither have started nor stared. She would have had her answer ready beforehand in her own mind, in case of accidents. There's only one thing in my experience that you can never do with a thief, when a thief happens to be a woman – you can never take her by surprise. Put that remark by in your mind; one day you may find a use for remembering it. Did you see her blush, and look quite hurt in her feelings, pretty dèar, when I asked about her sweetheart? Do you think a thief, in her place, would have shown such a face as that? Not she! The thief would have been relieved. The thief would have said to herself, "All right! the more the old fool talks about sweethearts the further he is from tracing the robbery to Me!" Yes! yes! the ground's cleared now, Master Moody. I've reckoned up the servants; I've questioned Miss Isabel; I've made my inquiries in all the other quarters that may be useful to us – and what's the result? The advice I gave, when you and the lawyer first came to me – I hate that fellow! – remains as sound and good advice as ever. I have got the thief in my mind,' said Old Sharon, closing his cunning eyes and then opening them again, 'as plain as I've got you in my eye at this minute. No more of that now,' he went on, looking round sharply at the path that led to the farm-house. I've something particular to say to you – and there's barely time to say it before that nice girl comes back. Look here! Do you happen to be acquainted with Mr-Honourable-Hardyman's valet?'

Moody's eyes rested on Old Sharon with a searching and doubtful look.

'Mr Hardyman's valet?' he repeated. 'I wasn't prepared to hear Mr Hardyman's name.'

Old Sharon looked at Moody, in his turn, with a flash of sardonic triumph.

'Oho!' he said. 'Has my good boy learnt his lesson? Do you

see the thief through my spectacles, already?'

'I began to see him,' Moody answered, 'when you gave us the guinea opinion at your lodgings.'

'Will you whisper his name?' asked Old Sharon.

'Not yet. I distrust my own judgment. I wait till time proves that you are right.'

Old Sharon knitted his shaggy brows and shook his head. 'If you had only a little more dash and go in you,' he said, 'you would be a clever fellow. As it is —— !' He finished the sentence by snapping his fingers with a grin of contempt. 'Let's get to business. Are you going back by the next train along with me? or are you going to stop with the young lady?'

'I will follow you by a later train,' Moody answered.

'Then I must give you my instructions at once,' Sharon continued. 'You get better acquainted with Hardyman's valet. Lend him money if he wants it – stick at nothing to make a bosom friend of him. I can't do that part of it; my appearance would be against me. *You* are the man – you are respectable from the top of your hat to the tips of your boots; nobody would suspect You. Don't make objections! Can you fix the valet? Or can't you?'

'I can try,' said Moody. 'And what then?'

Old Sharon put his gross lips disagreeably close to Moody's ear.

'Your friend the valet can tell you who his master's bankers are,' he said; 'and he can supply you with a specimen of his master's handwriting.'

Moody drew back, as suddenly as if his vagabond companion had put a knife to his throat. 'You old villain!' he said. 'Are you tempting me to forgery?'

'You infernal fool!' retorted Old Sharon. '*Will* you hold that long tongue of yours, and hear what I have to say. You go to Hardyman's bankers, with a note in Hardyman's handwriting (exactly imitated by me) to this effect: – "Mr H. presents his compliments to Messrs So-and-So, and is not quite certain whether a payment of five hundred pounds has been made within the last week to his account. He will be much obliged if Messrs So-and-So will inform him by a line in reply, whether there is such an entry to his credit in their books, and by whom the payment has been made." You wait for the bankers' answer, and bring it to me. It's just possible that the name you're afraid to whisper may appear in the letter. If it does, we've caught our man. Is *that* forgery, Mr Muddlehead Moody? I'll tell you what – if I had lived to be your age, and knew no more of the world than you do, I'd go and hang myself. Steady! here's our charming friend with the milk. Remember your instructions, and don't lose heart if my notion of the payment to the bankers comes to nothing. I know what to do next, in that case – and, what's more, I'll take all the risk and trouble on my own shoulders. Oh, Lord! I'm afraid I shall be obliged to drink the milk, now it's come!'

With this apprehension in his mind, he advanced to relieve Isabel of the jug that she carried.

'Here's a treat!' he burst out, with an affectation of joy, which was completely belied by the expression of his dirty face. 'Here's a kind and dear young lady, to help an old man to a drink with her own pretty hands.' He paused, and looked at the milk very much as he might have looked at a dose of physic. 'Will anyone take a drink first?' he asked, offering the jug piteously to Isabel and Moody. 'You see, I'm not used to genuine milk; I'm used to chalk and water. I don't know what effect the unadulterated cow might have on my poor old inside.' He tasted the milk with the greatest caution. 'Upon my soul, this is too rich for me! The unadulterated cow is a deal too strong to be drunk alone. If you'll allow me, I'll qualify it with a drop of gin. Here, Puggy, Puggy!' He set the milk down before the dog; and, taking a flask out of his pocket, emptied it at a draught. 'That's something like!' he said, smacking his lips with an air of infinite relief. 'So sorry, Miss, to have given you all your trouble for nothing; it's my ignorance that's to blame, not me. I couldn't know I was unworthy of genuine milk till I tried – could I? And do you know,' he proceeded, with his eyes directed slyly on the way back to the station, 'I begin to think I'm not worthy of the fresh air, either. A kind of longing seems to come over me for the London stink. I'm home-sick already for the soot of my happy childhood and my own dear native mud. The air here is too thin for me, and the sky's too clean; and – oh, Lord! – when you're used to the roar of the traffic – the 'busses and the cabs and what not – the silence in these parts is downright awful. I'll wish you good evening, Miss; and get back to London.'

Isabel turned to Moody with disappointment plainly expressed in her face and manner.

'Is that all he has to say?' she asked. 'You told me he could help us. You led me to suppose he could find the guilty person.'

Sharon heard her. 'I could name the guilty person,' he answered, 'as easily, Miss, as I could name you.'

'Why don't you do it, then?' Isabel inquired, not very patiently.

'Because the time's not ripe for it yet, Miss – that's one reason. Because, if I mentioned the thief's name, as things are now, you, Miss Isabel, would think me mad; and you would tell Mr Moody I had cheated him out of his money – that's another reason. The matter's in train, if you will only wait a little longer.'

'So you say,' Isabel rejoined. 'If you really could name the thief, I believe you would do it now.'

She turned away with a frown on her pretty face. Old Sharon followed her. Even his coarse sensibilities appeared to feel the irresistible ascendancy of beauty and youth.

'I say!' he began, 'we must part friends, you know – or I shall break my heart over it. They have got milk at the farm-house. Do you think they have got pen, ink, and paper too?'

Isabel answered, without turning to look at him, 'Of course they have!'

'And a bit of sealing-wax?'

'I dare say!'

Old Sharon laid his dirty claws on her shoulder and forced her to face him as the best means of shaking them off.

'Come along!' he said. 'I am going to pacify you with some information in writing.'

'Why should you write it?' Isabel asked suspiciously.

'Because I mean to make my own conditions, my dear, before I let you into the secret.'

In ten minutes more they were all three in the farm-house parlour. Nobody but the farmer's wife was at home. The good woman trembled from head to foot at the sight of Old

Sharon. In all her harmless life she had never yet seen humanity under the aspect in which it was now presented to her. 'Mercy preserve us, Miss!' she whispered to Isabel, 'how come you to be in such company as *that*?' Instructed by Isabel, she produced the necessary materials for writing and sealing – and, that done, she shrank away to the door. 'Please to excuse me, Miss,' she said with a last horrified look at her venerable visitor; 'I really can't stand the sight of such a blot of dirt as that in my nice clean parlour.' With those words she disappeared, and was seen no more.

Perfectly indifferent to his reception, Old Sharon wrote; inclosed what he had written in an envelope; and sealed it (in the absence of anything better fitted for his purpose) with the mouth-piece of his pipe.

'Now, Miss,' he said, 'you give me your word of honour' – he stopped and looked round at Moody with a grin – 'and you give me yours, that you won't either of you break the seal on this envelope till the expiration of one week from the present day. There are the conditions, Miss Isabel, on which I'll give you your information. If you stop to dispute with me, the candle's alight, and I'll burn it!'

It was useless to contend with him. Isabel and Moody gave him the promise that he required. He handed the sealed envelope to Isabel with a low bow. 'When the week's out,' he said, 'you will own I'm a cleverer fellow than you think me now. Wish you good evening, Miss. Come along, Puggy! Farewell to the horrid clean country, and back again to the nice London stink!'

He nodded to Moody – he leered at Isabel – he chuckled to himself – he left the farm-house.

CHAPTER XV

Isabel looked down at the letter in her hand – considered it in silence – and turned to Moody. 'I feel tempted to open it already,' she said.

'After giving your promise?' Moody gently remonstrated.

Isabel met that objection with a woman's logic.

'Does a promise matter?' she asked, 'when one gives it to a dirty, disreputable, presuming old wretch like Mr Sharon? It's a wonder to me that you trust such a creature. *I* wouldn't!'

'I doubted him just as you do,' Moody answered, 'when I first saw him in company with Mr Troy. But there was something in the advice he gave us at that first consultation which altered my opinion of him for the better. I dislike his appearance and his manners as much as you do – I may even say I felt ashamed of bringing such a person to see you. And yet I can't think that I have acted unwisely in employing Mr Sharon.'

Isabel listened absently. She had something more to say, and she was considering how she should say it. 'May I ask you a bold question?' she began.

'Any question you like.'

'Have you —— ' she hesitated and looked embarrassed. 'Have you paid Mr Sharon much money?' she resumed, suddenly rallying her courage. Instead of answering, Moody suggested that it was time to think of returning to Miss Pink's villa. 'Your aunt may be getting anxious about you.' he said.

Isabel led the way out of the farm-house in silence. She reverted to Mr Sharon and the money, however, as they returned by the path across the fields.

'I am sure you will not be offended with me,' she said gently, 'if I own that I am uneasy about the expense. I am allowing you to use your purse as if it was mine – and I have hardly any savings of my own.'

Moody entreated her not to speak of it. 'How can I put my money to a better use than in serving your interests?' he asked. 'My one object in life is to relieve you of your present anxieties. I shall be the happiest man living if you only owe a moment's happiness to my exertions!'

Isabel took his hand, and looked at him with grateful tears in her eyes.

'How good you are to me, Mr Moody!' she said. 'I wish I could tell you how deeply I feel your kindness.'

'You can do it easily,' he answered, with a smile. 'Call me "Robert" – don't call me "Mr Moody".'

She took his arm with a sudden familiarity that charmed him.

'If you had been my brother I should have called you "Robert",' she said; 'and no brother could have been more devoted to me than you are.'

He looked eagerly at her bright face turned up to his. 'May I never hope to be something nearer and dearer to you than a brother?' he asked timidly.

She hung her head, and said nothing. Moody's memory recalled Sharon's coarse reference to her 'sweetheart'. She had blushed when he put the question? What had she done when Moody put *his* question? Her face answered for her – she had turned pale; she was looking more serious than usual. Ignorant as he was of the ways of women, his instinct told him that this was a bad sign. Surely her rising colour would have confessed it, if time and gratitude together were teaching her to love him? He sighed as the inevitable conclusion forced itself on his mind.

'I hope I have not offended you?' he said sadly.

'Oh, no.'

'I wish I had not spoken. Pray don't think that I am serving you with any selfish motive.'

'I don't think that, Robert. I never could think it of *you*.'

He was not quite satisfied yet. 'Even if you were to marry some other man,' he went on earnestly, 'it would make no difference in what I am trying to do for you. No matter what I might suffer, I should still go on – for your sake.'

'Why do you talk so?' she burst out passionately. 'No other man has such a claim as you to my gratitude and regard. How can you let such thoughts come to you? I have done nothing in secret. I have no friends who are not known to you. Be satisfied with that, Robert – and let us drop the subject.'

'Never to take it up again?' he asked, with the infatuated pertinacity of a man clinging to his last hope.

At other times and under other circumstances, Isabel might have answered him sharply. She spoke with perfect gentleness now.

'Not for the present,' she said. 'I don't know my own heart. Give me time.'

His gratitude caught at those words, as the drowning man is said to catch at the proverbial straw. He lifted her hand, and suddenly and fondly pressed his lips on it. She showed no confusion. Was she sorry for him, poor wretch! – and was that all?

They walked on, arm-in-arm, in silence.

Crossing the last field, they entered again on the high road leading to the row of villas in which Miss Pink lived. The minds of both were preoccupied. Neither of them noticed a gentleman approaching on horseback, followed by a mounted groom. He was advancing slowly, at the walking-pace of his horse, and he only observed the two foot-passengers when he was close to them.

'Miss Isabel!'

She started, looked up, and discovered – Alfred Hardyman.

He was dressed in a perfectly-made travelling suit of light brown, with a peaked felt hat of a darker shade of the same colour, which, in a picturesque sense, greatly improved his personal appearance. His pleasure at discovering Isabel gave the animation to his features which they wanted on ordinary occasions. He sat his horse, a superb hunter, easily and gracefully. His light amber-coloured gloves fitted him perfectly. His obedient servant, on another magnificent horse, waited behind him. He looked the impersonation of rank and breeding – of wealth and prosperity. What a contrast, in a woman's eyes, to the shy, pale, melancholy man, in the ill-fitting black clothes, with the wandering uneasy glances, who stood beneath him, and felt, and showed that he felt, his inferior position keenly! In spite of herself, the treacherous blush flew over Isabel's face, in Moody's presence, and with Moody's eyes distrustfully watching her.

'This is a piece of good fortune that I hardly hoped for,' said Hardyman, his cool, quiet, dreary way of speaking quickened, as usual, in Isabel's presence. 'I only got back from France this morning, and I called on Lady Lydiard in the hope of seeing you. She was not at home – and you were in the country – and the servants didn't know the address. I could get nothing out of them, except that you were on a visit to a relation.' He looked at Moody while he was speaking. 'Haven't I seen you before?' he said carelessly. 'Yes; at Lady Lydiard's. You're her steward, are you not? How d'ye do?' Moody, with his eyes on the ground, answered silently by a bow. Hardyman, perfectly indifferent whether Lady Lydiard's steward spoke or not, turned on his saddle and looked admiringly at Isabel. 'I begin to think I am a lucky man at last,' he went on with a smile. 'I was jogging along to my farm, and despairing of ever seeing Miss Isabel again – and Miss Isabel herself meets me at the roadside! I wonder whether you are as glad to see me as I am to see you? You won't tell me – eh? May I ask you something-else? Are you staying in our neighbourhood?'

There was no alternative before Isabel but to answer this last question. Hardyman had met her out walking, and had no doubt drawn the inevitable inference – although he was too polite to say so in plain words.

'Yes, sir,' she answered shyly, 'I am staying in this neigh-bourhood.'

'And who is your relation?' Hardyman proceeded, in his easy, matter-of-course way. 'Lady Lydiard told me, when I had the pleasure of meeting you at her house, that you had an aunt living in the country. I have a good memory, Miss Isabel, for anything that I hear about You! It's your aunt, isn't it? Yes? I know everybody about here. What is your aunt's name?'

Isabel, still resting her hand on Robert's arm, felt it tremble a little as Hardyman made this last inquiry. If she had been speaking to one of her equals she would have known how to dispose of the question without directly answering it. But what could she say to the magnificent gentleman on the stately horse? He had only to send his servant into the village to ask who the young lady from London was staying with, and the answer, in a dozen mouths at least, would direct him to her aunt. She cast one appealing look at Moody and pronounced the distinguished name of Miss Pink.

'Miss Pink?' Hardyman repeated. 'Surely I know Miss Pink?' (He had not the faintest remembrances of her.) 'Where did I meet her last?' (He ran over in his memory the different local festivals at which strangers had been introduced to him.) 'Was it at the archery meeting? or at the grammar-school when the prizes were given? No? It must have been at the flower show, then, surely?'

It *had* been at the flower show. Isabel had heard it from Miss Pink fifty times at least, and was obliged to admit it now.

'I am quite ashamed of never having called,' Hardyman

proceeded. 'The fact is, I have so much to do. I am a bad one at paying visits. Are you on your way home? Let me follow you and make my apologies personally to Miss Pink.'

Moody looked at Isabel. It was only a momentary glance, but she perfectly understood it.

'I am afraid, sir, my aunt cannot have the honour of seeing you to-day,' she said.

Hardyman was all compliance. He smiled and patted his horse's neck. 'To-morrow, then,' he said. 'My compliments, and I will call in the afternoon. Let me see: Miss Pink lives at ——?' He waited, as if he expected Isabel to assist his treacherous memory once more. She hesitated again. Hardyman looked round at his groom. The groom could find out the address, even if he did not happen to know it already. Besides, there was the little row of houses visible at the farther end of the road. Isabel pointed to the villas, as a necessary concession to good manners, before the groom could anticipate her. 'My aunt lives there, sir; at the house called The Lawn.'

'Ah! to be sure!' said Hardyman. 'I oughtn't to have wanted reminding; but I have so many things to think of at the farm. And I am afraid I must be getting old – my memory isn't as good as it was. I am so glad to have seen you, Miss Isabel. You and your aunt must come and look at my horses. Do you like horses? Are you fond of riding? I have a quiet roan mare that is used to carrying ladies; she would be just the thing for you. Did I beg you to give my best compliments to your aunt? Yes? How well you are looking! our air here agrees with you. I hope I haven't kept you standing too long? I didn't think of it in the pleasure of meeting you. Good-bye, Miss Isabel; good-bye, till to-morrow!'

He took off his hat to Isabel, nodded to Moody, and pursued his way to the farm.

Isabel looked at her companion. His eyes were still on the ground. Pale, silent, motionless, he waited by her like a dog, until she gave the signal of walking on again towards the house.

'You are not angry with me for speaking to Mr Hardyman?' she asked anxiously.

He lifted his head at the sound of her voice. 'Angry with you, my dear! why should I be angry?'

'You seem so changed, Robert, since we met Mr Hardyman. I couldn't help speaking to him – could I?'

'Certainly not.'

They moved on towards the villa. Isabel was still uneasy. There was something in Moody's silent submission to all that she said and all that she did which pained and humiliated her. 'You're not jealous?' she said, smiling timidly.

He tried to speak lightly on his side. 'I have no time to be jealous while I have your affairs to look after,' he answered.

She pressed his arm tenderly. 'Never fear, Robert, that new friends will make me forget the best and dearest friend who is now at my side.' She paused, and looked up at him with a compassionate fondness that was very pretty to see. 'I can keep out of the way to-morrow, when Mr Hardyman calls,' she said. 'It is my aunt he is coming to see – not me.'

It was generously meant. But while her mind was only occupied with the present time, Moody's mind was looking into the future. He was learning the hard lesson of self-sacrifice already. 'Do what you think is right,' he said quietly; 'don't think of me.'

They reached the gate of the villa. He held out his hand to say good-bye.

'Won't you come in?' she asked. 'Do come in!'

'Not now, my dear. I must get back to London as soon as I can. There is some more work to be done for you, and the sooner I do it the better.'

She heard his excuse without heeding it.

'You are not like yourself, Robert,' she said. 'Why is it? What are you thinking of?'

He was thinking of the bright blush that overspread her face when Hardyman first spoke to her; he was thinking of the invitation to her to see the stud-farm, and to ride the roan mare; he was thinking of the utterly powerless position in which he stood towards Isabel and towards the highly-born gentleman who admired her. But he kept his doubts and fears to himself. 'The train won't wait for me,' he said, and held out his hand once more.

She was not only perplexed; she was really distressed. 'Don't take leave of me in that cold way!' she pleaded. Her eyes dropped before his, and her lips trembled a little. 'Give me a kiss, Robert, at parting.' She said those bold words softly and sadly, out of the depth of her pity for him! He started; his face brightened suddenly; his sinking hope rose again. In another moment the change came; in another moment he understood her. As he touched her cheek with his lips, he turned pale again. 'Don't quite forget me,' he said, in low faltering tones – and left her.

Miss Pink met Isabel in the hall. Refreshed by unbroken repose, the ex-schoolmistress was in the happiest frame of mind for the reception of her niece's news.

Informed that Moody had travelled to South Morden to personally report the progress of the inquiries, Miss Pink highly approved of him as a substitute for Mr Troy. 'Mr Moody, as a banker's son, is a gentleman by birth,' she remarked; 'he has condescended, in becoming Lady Lydiard's steward. What I saw of him, when he came here with you, prepossessed me in his favour. He has my confidence, Isabel, as well as yours – he is in every respect a superior person to Mr Troy. Did you meet any friends, my dear, when you were out walking?'

The answer to this question produced a species of transformation in Miss Pink. The rapturous rank-worship of her nation feasted, so to speak, on Hardyman's message. She looked taller and younger than usual – she was all smiles and sweetness. 'At last, Isabel, you have seen birth and breeding under their right aspect,' she said. 'In the society of Lady Lydiard, you cannot possibly have formed correct ideas of the English aristocracy. Observe Mr Hardyman when he does me the honour to call to-morrow – and you will see the difference.'

'Mr Hardyman is your visitor, aunt – not mine. I was going to ask you to let me remain upstairs in my room.'

Miss Pink was unaffectedly shocked. 'This is what you learn at Lady Lydiard's!' she observed. 'No, Isabel, your absence would be a breach of good manners – I cannot possibly permit it. You will be present to receive our distinguished friend with me. And mind this!' added Miss Pink, in her most impressive manner, 'If Mr Hardyman should by any chance ask why you have left Lady Lydiard, not one word about those disgraceful circumstances which connect you with the loss of the bank-note! I should sink into the earth if the smallest hint of what has really happened should reach Mr Hardyman's ears. My child, I stand towards you in the place of your lamented mother; I have the right to command your silence on this horrible subject, and I do imperatively command it.'

In these words foolish Miss Pink sowed the seed for the harvest of trouble that was soon come.

CHAPTER XVI

Paying his court to the ex-schoolmistress on the next day, Hardyman made such excellent use of his opportunities that the visit to the stud-farm took place on the day after. His own carriage was placed at the disposal of Isabel and her aunt; and his own sister was present to confer special distinction on the reception of Miss Pink.

In a country like England, which annually suspends the sitting of its Legislature in honour of a horse-race, it is only natural and proper that the comfort of the horses should be the first object of consideration at a stud-farm. Nine tenths of the land at Hardyman's farm was devoted, in one way or another, to the noble quadruped with the low forehead and the long nose. Poor humanity was satisfied with second-rate and third-rate accommodation. The ornamental grounds, very poorly laid out, were also very limited in extent – and, as for the dwelling-house, it was literally a cottage. A parlour and a kitchen, a smoking-room, a bed-room, and a spare chamber for a friend, all scantily furnished, sufficed for the modest wants of the owner of the property. If you wished to feast your eyes on luxury you went to the stables.

The stud-farm being described, the introduction to Hardyman's sister follows in due course.

The Honourable Lavinia Hardyman was, as all persons in society know, married rather late in life to General Drumblade. It is saying a great deal, but it is not saying too much, to describe Mrs Drumblade as the most mischievous woman of her age in all England. Scandal was the breath of her life; to place people in false positions, to divulge secrets and destroy characters, to undermine friendships, and aggravate enmities – these were the sources of enjoyment from which this danger-ous woman drew the inexhaustible fund of good spirits that made her a brilliant light in the social sphere. She was one of the privileged sinners of modern society. The worst mischief that she could work was ascribed to her 'exuberant vitality'. She had that ready familiarity of manner which is (in *her* class) so rarely discovered to be insolence in disguise. Her power of easy self-assertion found people ready to accept her on her own terms wherever she went. She was one of those big, overpowering women, with blunt manners, voluble tongues, and goggle eyes, who carry everything before them. The highest society modestly considered itself in danger of being dull in the absence of Mrs Drumblade. Even Hardyman himself – who saw as little of her as possible, whose frankly straightforward nature recoiled by instinct from contact with his sister – could think of no fitter person to make Miss Pink's reception agreeable to her, while he was devoting his own attentions to her niece. Mrs Drumblade accepted the position thus offered with the most amiable readiness. In her own private mind she placed an interpretation on her brother's motives which did him the grossest injustice. She believed that Hardyman's designs on Isabel contemplated the most proflig-ate result. To assist this purpose, while the girl's nearest relative was supposed to be taking care of her, was Mrs Drumblade's idea of 'fun'. Her worst enemies admitted that the Honourable Lavinia had redeeming qualities, and owned that a keen sense of humour was one of her merits.

Was Miss Pink a likely person to resist the fascinations of Mrs Drumblade? Alas, for the ex-schoolmistress! Before she had been five minutes at the farm, Hardyman's sister had fished for her, caught her, landed her. Poor Miss Pink!

Mrs Drumblade could assume a grave dignity of manner when the occasion called for it. She was grave, she was dignified, when Hardyman performed the ceremonies of introduction. She would not say she was charmed to meet Miss Pink – the ordinary slang of society was not for Miss Pink's ears – she would say she felt this introduction as a privilege. It was so seldom one met with persons of trained intellect in society. Mrs Drumblade was already informed of Miss Pink's earlier triumphs in the instruction of youth. Mrs Drumblade had not been blessed with children herself; but she had nephews and nieces, and she was anxious about their education, especially the nieces. What a sweet, modest girl Miss Isabel was! The fondest wish she could form for her nieces would be that they should resemble Miss Isabel when they grew up. The question was, as to the best method of education. She would own that she had selfish motives in becoming acquainted with Miss Pink. They were at the farm, no doubt, to see Alfred's horses. Mrs Drumblade did not understand horses; her interest was in the question of education. She might even confess that she had accepted Alfred's invitation in the hope of hearing Miss Pink's views. There would be opportunities, she trusted, for a little instructive conversation on that subject. It was, perhaps, ridiculous to talk, at her age, of feeling as if she was Miss Pink's pupil; and yet it exactly expressed the nature of the aspiration which was then in her mind. In these terms, feeling her way with the utmost nicety, Mrs Drumblade wound the net of flattery round and round Miss Pink until her hold on that innocent lady was, in every sense of the word, secure. Before half the horses had been passed under review, Hardyman and Isabel were out of sight, and Mrs Drumblade and Miss Pink were lost in the intricacies of the stables. 'Excessively stupid of me! We had better go back, and establish ourselves comfortably in the parlour. When my brother misses us, he and your charming niece will return to look for us in the cottage.' Under cover of this arrangement the separation became complete. Miss Pink held forth on education to Mrs Drumblade in the parlour; while Hardyman and Isabel were on their way to a paddock at the farthest limits of the property.

'I am afraid you are getting a little tired,' said Hardyman. 'Won't you take my arm?'

Isabel was on her guard: she had not forgotten what Lady Lydiard had said to her. 'No, thank you, Mr Hardyman; I am a better walker than you think.'

Hardyman continued the conversation in his blunt, resolute way. 'I wonder whether you will believe me,' he asked, 'if I tell you that this is one of the happiest days of my life.'

'I should think you were always happy,' Isabel cautiously replied, 'having such a pretty place to live in as this.'

Hardyman met that answer with one of his quietly-positive denials. 'A man is never happy by himself,' he said. 'He is happy with a companion. For instance, I am happy with you.'

Isabel stopped and looked back. Hardyman's language was becoming a little too explicit. 'Surely we have lost Mrs Drumblade and my aunt,' she said. 'I don't see them anywhere.'

'You will see them directly; they are only a long way behind.' With this assurance, he returned, in his own obstinate way, to his one object in view. 'Miss Isabel, I want to ask you a question. I'm not a ladies' man. I speak my mind plainly to everybody – women included. Do you like being here to-day?'

Isabel's gravity was not proof against this very downright question. 'I should be hard to please,' she said laughing, 'if I didn't enjoy my visit to the farm.'

Hardyman pushed steadily forward through the obstacle of the farm to the question of the farm's master. 'You like being her,' he repeated. 'Do you like Me?'

This was serious. Isabel drew back a little, and looked at him. He waited with the most impenetrable gravity for her reply.

'I think you can hardly expect me to answer that question,' she said.

'Why not?'

'Our acquaintance has been a very short one, Mr Hardyman. And, if *you* are so good as to forget the difference between us, I think *I* ought to remember it.'

'What difference?'

'The difference in rank.'

Hardyman suddenly stood still, and emphasized his next words by digging his stick into the grass.

'If anything I have said has vexed you,' he began, 'tell me so plainly, Miss Isabel, and I'll ask your pardon. But don't throw my rank in my face. I cut adrift from all that nonsense when I took this farm and got my living out of the horses. What has a man's rank to do with a man's feelings?' he went on, with another emphatic dig of his stick. 'I am quite serious in asking if you like me – for this good reason, that I like you. Yes, I do. You remember that day when I bled the old lady's dog – well, I have found out since then that there's a sort of incompleteness in my life which I never suspected before. It's you who have put that idea into my head. You didn't mean it, I dare say, but you have done it all the same. I sat alone here yesterday evening smoking my pipe – and I didn't enjoy it. I breakfasted alone this morning – and I didn't enjoy *that*. I said to myself, She's coming to lunch, that's one comfort – I shall enjoy lunch. That's what I feel, roughly described. I don't suppose I've been five minutes together without thinking of you, now in one way and now in another, since the day when I first saw you. When a man comes to my time of life, and has had any experience, he knows what that means. It means, in plain English, that his heart is set on a woman. You're the woman.'

Isabel had thus far made several attempts to interrupt him, without success. But, when Hardyman's confession attained its culminating point, she insisted on being heard.

'If you will excuse me, sir,' she interposed gravely, 'I think I had better go back to the cottage. My aunt is a stranger here, and she doesn't know where to look for us.'

'We don't want your aunt,' Hardyman remarked, in his most positive manner.

'We do want her,' Isabel rejoined. 'I won't venture to say it's wrong in you, Mr Hardyman, to talk to me as you have just done, but I am quite sure it's very wrong of me to listen.'

He looked at her with such unaffected surprise and distress that she stopped, on the point of leaving him, and tried to make herself better understood.

'I had no intention of offending you, sir,' she said, a little confusedly. 'I only wanted to remind you that there are some things which a gentleman in your position ——' She stopped, tried to finish the sentence, failed, and began another. 'If I had been a young lady in your own rank of life,' she went on, 'I might have thanked you for paying me a compliment, and have given you a serious answer. As it is, I am afraid that I must say that you have surprised and disappointed me. I can claim very little for myself, I know. But I did imagine – so long as there was nothing unbecoming in my conduct – that I had some right to your respect.'

Listening more and more impatiently, Hardyman took her by the hand, and burst out with another of his abrupt questions.

'What can you possibly be thinking of?' he asked.

She gave him no answer; she only looked at him reproachfully, and tried to release herself.

Hardyman held her hand faster than ever.

'I believe you think me an infernal scoundrel!' he said. 'I can stand a good deal, Miss Isabel, but I can't stand *that*. How have I failed in respect toward you, if you please? I have told you you're the woman my heart is set on. Well? Isn't it plain what I want of you, when I say that? Isabel Miller, I want you to be my wife!'

Isabel's only reply to this extraordinary proposal of marriage was a faint cry of astonishment, followed by a sudden trembling that shook her from head to foot.

Hardyman put his arm round her with a gentleness which his oldest friend would have been surprised to see in him.

'Take your time to think of it,' he said, dropping back again into his usual quiet tone. 'If you had known me a little better you wouldn't have mistaken me, and you wouldn't be looking at me now as if you were afraid to believe your own ears. What is there so very wonderful in my wanting to marry you? I don't set up for being a saint. When I was a younger man I was no better (and no worse) than other young men. I'm getting on now to middle life. I don't want romances and adventures – I want an easy existence with a nice lovable woman who will make me a good wife. You're the woman, I tell you again. I know it by what I've seen of you myself, and by what I have heard of you from Lady Lydiard. She said you were prudent, and sweet-tempered, and affectionate; to which I wish to add that you have just the face and figure that I like, and the modest manners and the blessed absence of all slang in your talk, which I don't find in the young women I meet with in the present day. That's my view of it: I think for myself. What does it matter to me whether you're the daughter of a Duke or the daughter of a Dairyman? It isn't your father I want to marry – it's you. Listen to reason, there's a dear! We have only one question to settle before we go back to your aunt. You wouldn't answer me when I asked it a little while since. Will you answer now? *Do* you like me?'

Isabel looked up at him timidly.

'In my position, sir,' she asked, 'have I any right to like you? What would your relations and friends think, if I said Yes?'

Hardyman gave her waist a little admonitory squeeze with his arm.

'What? You're at it again? A nice way to answer a man, to call him "Sir", and to get behind his rank as if it was a place of refuge from him! I hate talking of myself, but you force me to it. Here is my position in the world – I have got an elder brother; he is married, and he has a son to succeed him in the title and the property. You understand, so far? Very well! Years ago I shifted my share of the rank (whatever it may be) on to my brother's shoulders. He is a thorough good fellow, and he has carried my dignity for me, without once dropping it, ever since. As for what people may say, they have said it already, from my father and mother downwards, in the time when I took to the horses and the farm. If they're the wise people I take them for, they won't be at the trouble of saying it all over again. No, no. Twist it how you may, Miss Isabel, whether I'm single or whether I'm married, I'm plain Alfred Hardyman; and everybody who knows me knows that I go on my way, and please myself. If you don't like me, it will be the bitterest disappointment I ever had in my life; but say so honestly, all the same.'

Where is the woman in Isabel's place whose capacity for resistance would not have yielded a little to such an appeal as this?

'I should be an insensible wretch,' she replied warmly, 'if I didn't feel the honour you have done me, and feel it gratefully.'

'Does that mean you will have me for a husband?' asked downright Hardyman.

She was fairly driven into a corner; but (being a woman) she tried to slip through his fingers at the last moment.

'Will you forgive me,' she said, 'if I ask you for a little more time? I am so bewildered, I hardly know what to say or do for the best. You see, Mr Hardyman, it would be a dreadful thing for me to be the cause of giving offence to your family. I am obliged to think of that. It would be so distressing for you (I will say nothing of myself) if your friends closed their doors on me. They might say I was a designing girl, who had taken advantage of your good opinion to raise herself in the world. Lady Lydiard warned me long since not to be ambitious about myself and not to forget my station in life, because she treated me like her adopted daughter. Indeed – indeed, I can't tell you how I feel your goodness, and the compliment – the very great compliment, you pay me! My heart is free; and if I followed my own inclinations —— ' She checked herself, conscious that she was on the brink of saying too much. 'Will you give me a few days,' she pleaded, 'to try if I can think composedly of all this? I am only a girl, and I feel quite dazzled by the prospect that you set before me.'

Hardyman seized on those words as offering all the encouragement that he desired to his suit.

'Have your own way in this thing and in everything!' he said, with an unaccustomed fervour of language and manner. 'I am so glad to hear that your heart is open to me, and that all your inclinations take my part.'

Isabel instantly protested against this misrepresentation of what she had really said, 'Oh, Mr Hardyman, you quite mistake me!'

He answered her very much as he had answered Lady Lydiard, when she had tried to make him understand his proper relations towards Isabel.

'No, no; I don't mistake you. I agree to every word you say. How can I expect you to marry me, as you very properly remark, unless I give you a day or two to make up your mind? It's quite enough for me that you like the prospect. If Lady Lydiard treated you as her daughter, why shouldn't you be my wife? It stands to reason that you're quite right to marry a man who can raise you in the world. I like you to be ambitious – though Heaven knows it isn't much I can do for you, except to love you with all my heart. Still, it's a great encouragement to hear that her Ladyship's views agree with mine ——'

'They don't agree, Mr Hardyman!' protested poor Isabel. 'You are entirely misrepresenting —— '

Hardyman cordially concurred in this view of the matter. 'Yes! yes! I can't pretend to represent her Ladyship's language, or yours either; I am obliged to take my words as they come to me. Don't disturb yourself: it's all right – I understand. You have made me the happiest man living. I shall ride over to-morrow to your aunt's house, and hear what you have to say to me. Mind you're at home! Not a day must pass now without my seeing you. I do love you, Isabel – I do indeed!' He stooped, and kissed her heartily. 'Only to reward me,' he explained, 'for giving you time to think.'

She drew herself away from him – resolutely, not angrily. Before she could make a third attempt to place the subject in its right light before him, the luncheon bell rang at the cottage – and a servant appeared, evidently sent to look for them.

'Don't forget to-morrow,' Hardyman whispered confidentially. 'I'll call early – and then go to London, and get the ring.'

CHAPTER XVII

Events succeeded each other rapidly, after the memorable day to Isabel of the luncheon at the farm.

On the next day (the ninth of the month) Lady Lydiard sent for her steward, and requested him to explain his conduct in repeatedly leaving the house without assigning any reason for his absence. She did not dispute his claims to a freedom of action which would not be permitted to an ordinary servant. Her objection to his present course of proceeding related entirely to the mystery in which it was involved, and to the uncertainty in which the household was left as to the hour of his return. On those grounds, she thought herself entitled to an explanation. Moody's habitual reserve – strengthened, on this occasion, by his dread of ridicule, if his efforts to serve Isabel ended in failure – disinclined him to take Lady Lydiard into his confidence, while his inquiries were still beset with obstacles and doubts. He respectfully entreated her Ladyship to grant him a delay of a few weeks before he entered on his explanation. Lady Lydiard's quick temper resented his request. She told Moody plainly that he was guilty of an act of presumption in making his own conditions with his employer. He received the reproof with exemplary resignation; but he held to his conditions nevertheless. From that moment the result of the interview was no longer in doubt. Moody was directed to send in his accounts. The accounts having been examined, and found to be scrupulously correct, he declined accepting the balance of salary that was offered to him. The next day he left Lady Lydiard's service.

On the tenth of the month her Ladyship received a letter from her nephew.

The health of Felix had not improved. He had made up his mind to go abroad again towards the end of the month. In the meantime, he had written to his friend in Paris, and he had the pleasure of forwarding an answer. The letter inclosed announced that the lost five-hundred-pound note had been made the subject of careful inquiry in Paris. It had not been traced. The French police offered to send to London one of their best men, well acquainted with the English language, if Lady Lydiard was desirous of employing him. He would be perfectly willing to act with an English officer in conducting the investigation, should it be thought necessary. Mr Troy being consulted as to the expediency of accepting this proposal, objected to the pecuniary terms demanded as being extravagantly high. He suggested waiting a little before any reply was sent to Paris; and he engaged meanwhile to consult a London solicitor who had great experience in cases of theft, and whose advice might enable them to dispense entirely with the services of the French police.

Being now a free man again, Moody was able to follow his own inclinations in regard to the instructions which he had received from Old Sharon.

The course that had been recommended to him was repellent to the self-respect and the sense of delicacy which were among the inbred virtues of Moody's character. He shrank from forcing himself as a friend on Hardyman's valet: he recoiled from the idea of tempting the man to steal a specimen of his master's handwriting. After some consideration, he decided on applying to the agent who collected the rents at Hardyman's London chambers. Being an old acquaintance of Moody's, this person would certainly not hesitate to communicate the address of Hardyman's bankers, if he knew it.

The experiment, tried under these favouring circumstances, proved perfectly successful. Moody proceeded to Sharon's lodgings the same day, with the address of the bankers in his pocket-book. The old vagabond, greatly amused by Moody's scruples, saw plainly enough that, so long as he wrote the supposed letter from Hardyman in the third person, it mattered little what handwriting was employed, seeing that no signature would be necessary. The letter was at once composed, on the model which Sharon had already suggested to Moody, and a respectable messenger (so far as outward appearances went) was employed to take it to the bank. In half an hour the answer came back. It added one more to the difficulties which beset the inquiry after the lost money. No such sum as five hundred pounds had been paid, within the dates mentioned, to the credit of Hardyman's account.

Old Sharon was not in the least discomposed by this fresh check. 'Give my love to the dear young lady,' he said with his customary impudence; 'and tell her we are one degree nearer to finding the thief.'

Moody looked at him, doubting whether he was in jest or in earnest.

'Must I squeeze a little more information into that thick head of yours?' asked Sharon. With this question he produced a weekly newspaper, and pointed to a paragraph which reported, among the items of sporting news, Hardyman's recent visit to a sale of horses at a town in the north of France. 'We know he didn't pay the bank-note in to his account,' Sharon remarked. 'What else did he do with it? Took it to pay for the horses that he bought in France! Do you see your way a little plainer now? Very good. Let's try next if your money holds out. Somebody must cross the Channel in search of the note. Which of us two is to sit in the steam-boat with a white basin on his lap? Old Sharon, of course!' He stopped to count the money still left, out of the sum deposited by Moody to defray the cost of the inquiry. 'All right!' he went on. 'I've got enough to pay my expenses there and back. Don't stir out of London till you hear from me. I can't tell how soon I may not want you. If there's any difficulty in tracing the note, your hand will have to go into your pocket again. Can't you get the lawyer to join you? Lord! how I should enjoy squandering *his* money! It's a downright disgrace to me to have only got one guinea out of him. I could tear my flesh off my bones when I think of it.'

The same night Old Sharon started for France, by way of Dover and Calais.

Two days elapsed, and brought no news from Moody's agent. On the third day, he received some information relating to Sharon – not from the man himself, but in a letter from Isabel Miller.

'For once, dear Robert,' she wrote, 'my judgment has turned out to be sounder than yours. That hateful old man has confirmed my worst opinion of him. Pray have him punished. Take him before a magistrate and charge him with cheating you out of your money. I enclose the sealed letter which he gave me at the farm-house. The week's time before I was to open it expired yesterday. Was there ever anything so impudent and so inhuman? I am too vexed and angry about the money you have wasted on this old wretch to write more. Yours, gratefully and affectionately, Isabel.'

The letter in which Old Sharon had undertaken (by way of pacifying Isabel) to write the name of the thief, contained these lines:

'You are a charming girl, my dear; but you still want one thing to make you perfect – and that is a lesson in patience. I am proud and happy to teach you. The name of the thief remains, for the present, Mr —— (Blank).'

From Moody's point of view, there was but one thing to be said of this: it was just like Old Sharon! Isabel's letter was of infinitely greater interest to him. He feasted his eyes on the words above the signature: she signed herself, 'Yours gratefully and affectionately.' Did the last words mean that she was really beginning to be fond of him? After kissing the word, he wrote a comforting letter to her, in which he pledged himself to keep a watchful eye on Sharon, and to trust him with no more money until he had honestly earned it first.

A week passed. Moody (longing to see Isabel) still waited in

vain for news from France. He had just decided to delay his
visit to South Morden no longer, when the errand-boy
employed by Sharon brought him this message: – 'The old
'un's at home, and waitin' to see yer.'

CHAPTER XVIII

Sharon's news was not of an encouraging character. He had
met with serious difficulties, and had spent the last farthing of
Moody's money in attempting to overcome them.

One discovery of importance he had certainly made. A
horse withdrawn from the sale was the only horse that had
met with Hardyman's approval. He had secured the animal at
the high reserved price of twelve thousand francs – being four
hundred and eighty pounds in English money; and he had paid
with an English bank-note. The seller (a French horse-dealer
resident in Brussels) had returned to Belgium immediately on
completing the negotiations. Sharon had ascertained his
address, and had written to him at Brussels, enclosing the
number of the lost bank-note. In two days he had received an
answer, informing him that the horse-dealer had been called to
England by the illness of a relative, and that he had hitherto
failed to send any address to which his letters could be
forwarded. Hearing this, and having exhausted his funds,
Sharon had returned to London. It now rested with Moody to
decide whether the course of the inquiry should follow the
horse-dealer next. Here was the cash account, showing how
the money had been spent. And there was Sharon, with his
pipe in his mouth and his dog on his lap, waiting for orders.

Moody wisely took time to consider before he committed
himself to a decision. In the meanwhile, he ventured to
recommend a new course of proceeding which Sharon's
report had suggested to his mind.

'It seems to me,' he said, 'that we have taken the round-
about way of getting to our end in view, when the straight
road lay before us. If Mr Hardyman has passed the stolen note,

you know, as well as I do, that he has passed it innocently. Instead of wasting time and money in trying to trace a stranger, why not tell Mr Hardyman what has happened, and ask him to give us the number of the note? You can't think of everything, I know; but it does seem strange that this idea didn't occur to you before you went to France.'

'Mr Moody,' said Old Sharon, 'I shall have to cut your acquaintance. You are a man without faith; I don't like you. As if I hadn't thought of Hardyman weeks since!' he exclaimed contemptuously. 'Are you really soft enough to suppose that a gentleman in his position would talk about his money affairs to me? You know mighty little of him if you do. A fortnight since I sent one of my men (most respectably dressed) to hang about his farm, and see what information he could pick up. My man became painfully acquainted with the toe of a boot. It was thick, sir; and it was Hardyman's.'

'I will run the risk of the boot,' Moody replied, in his quiet way.

'And put the question to Hardyman?'

'Yes.'

'Very good,' said Sharon. 'If you get your answer from his tongue, instead of his boot, the case is cleared up – unless I have made a complete mess of it. Look here, Moody! If you want to do me a good turn, tell the lawyer that the guinea-opinion was the right one. Let him know that *he* was the fool, not you, when he buttoned up his pockets and refused to trust me. And, I say,' pursued Old Sharon, relapsing into his customary impudence, 'you're in love, you know, with that nice girl. I like her myself. When you marry her invite me to the wedding. I'll make a sacrifice: I'll brush my hair and wash my face in honour of the occasion.'

Returning to his lodgings, Moody found two letters waiting on the table. One of them bore the South Morden postmark. He opened that letter first.

It was written by Miss Pink. The first lines contained an urgent entreaty to keep the circumstances connected with the loss of the five hundred pounds the strictest secret from everyone in general, and from Hardyman in particular. The reasons assigned for making the strange request were next expressed in these terms: – 'My niece Isabel is, I am happy to inform you, engaged to be married to Mr Hardyman. If the slightest hint reached him of her having been associated, no matter how cruelly and unjustly, with a suspicion of theft, the marriage would be broken off, and the result to herself and to everybody connected with her, would be disgrace for the rest of our lives.'

On the blank space at the foot of the page a few words were added in Isabel's writing: – 'Whatever changes there may be in my life, your place in my heart is one that no other person can fill: it is the place of my dearest friend. Pray write and tell me that you are not distressed and not angry. My one anxiety is that you should remember what I have always told you about the state of my own feelings. My one wish is that you will still let me love you and value you, as I might have loved and valued a brother.'

The letter dropped from Moody's hand. Not a word – not even a sigh – passed his lips. In tearless silence he submitted to the pang that wrung him. In tearless silence he contemplated the wreck of his life.

CHAPTER XIX

The narrative returns to South Morden, and follows the events which attended Isabel's marriage engagement.

To say that Miss Pink, inflated by the triumph, rose, morally speaking, from the earth and floated among the clouds, is to indicate faintly the effect produced on the ex-schoolmistress when her niece first informed her of what had happened at the farm. Attacked on one side by her aunt, and on the other by Hardyman, and feebly defended, at the best, by her own doubts and misgivings, Isabel ended by surrendering at discretion. Like thousands of other women in a similar position, she was in the last degree uncertain as to the state of her own heart. To what extent she was insensibly influenced by Hardyman's commanding position in believing herself to be sincerely attached to him, it was beyond her power of self-examination to discover. He doubly dazzled her by his birth and by his celebrity. Not in England only, but throughout Europe, he was a recognized authority on his own subject. How could she – how could any woman – resist the influence of his steady mind, his firmness of purpose, his manly resolution to owe everything to himself and nothing to his rank, set off as these attractive qualities were by the outward and personal advantages which exercise an ascendancy of their own? Isabel was fascinated, and yet Isabel was not at ease. In her lonely moments she was troubled by regreful thoughts of Moody, which perplexed and irritated her. She had always behaved honestly to him; she had never encouraged him to hope that his love for her had the faintest prospect of being returned. Yet, knowing, as she did, that her conduct was blameless so far, there were nevertheless perverse sympathies in her which took his part. In the wakeful hours of the night there were whispering voices in her which said, 'Think of Moody!' Had there been a growing kindness towards this good friend in her heart, of which she herself was not aware? She tried to detect it – to weigh it for what it was really worth. But it lay too deep to be discovered and estimated, if it did really exist – if it had any sounder origin than her own morbid fancy. In the broad light of day, in the little bustling duties of life, she forgot it again. She could think of what she ought to wear on the wedding day; she could even try privately how her new signature, 'Isabel Hardyman', would look when she had the right to use it. On the whole, it may be said that the time passed smoothly – with some occasional checks and drawbacks, which were the more easily endured seeing that they took their rise in Isabel's own conduct. Compliant as she was in general, there were two instances, among others, in which her resolution to take her own way was not to be overcome. She refused to write either to Moody or to Lady Lydiard informing them of her engagement; and she steadily disapproved of Miss Pink's policy of concealment, in the matter of the robbery at Lady Lydiard's house. Her aunt could only secure her as a passive accomplice by stating family considerations in the strongest possible terms. 'If the disgrace was confined to you, my dear, I might leave you to decide. But I am involved in it, as your nearest relative; and, what is more, even the sacred memories of your father and mother might feel the slur cast on them.' This exaggerated language – like all exaggerated language, a mischievous weapon in the arsenal of weakness and prejudice – had its effect on Isabel. Reluctantly and sadly, she consented to be silent.

Miss Pink wrote word of the engagement to Moody first; reserving to a later day the superior pleasure of informing Lady Lydiard of the very event which that audacious woman had declared to be impossible. To her aunt's surprise, just as she was about to close the envelope Isabel stepped forward, and inconsistently requested leave to add a postscript to the very letter which she had refused to write! Miss Pink was not even permitted to see the postscript. Isabel secured the envelope the moment she laid down her pen, and retired to her room with a headache (which was heartache in disguise) for the rest of the day.

While the question of marriage was still in debate, an event occurred which exercised a serious influence on Hardyman's future plans.

He received a letter from the Continent which claimed his immediate attention. One of the sovereigns of Europe had decided on making some radical changes in the mounting and equipment of a cavalry regiment; and he required the assistance of Hardyman in that important part of the contemplated reform which was connected with the choice and purchase of horses. Setting his own interests out of the question, Hardyman owed obligations to the kindness of his illustrious correspondent which made it possible for him to send an excuse. In a fortnight's time, at the latest, it would be necessary for him to leave England; and a month or more might elapse before it would be possible for him to return.

Under these circumstances, he proposed, in his own precipitate way, to hasten the date of the marriage. The necessary legal delay would permit the ceremony to be performed on that day fortnight. Isabel might then accompany him on his journey, and spend a brilliant honeymoon at the foreign Court. She at once refused, not only to accept his proposal, but even to take it into consideration. While Miss Pink dwelt eloquently on the shortness of the notice, Miss Pink's niece based her resolution on far more important grounds. Hardyman had not yet announced the contemplated marriage to his parents and friends; and Isabel was determined not to become his wife until she could be first assured of a courteous and tolerant reception by the family – if she could hope for no warmer welcome at their hands.

Hardyman was not a man who yielded easily, even in trifles. In the present case, his dearest interests were concerned in inducing Isabel to reconsider her decision. He was still vainly trying to shake her resolution, when the afternoon post brought a letter for Miss Pink which introduced a new element of disturbance into the discussion. The letter was nothing less than Lady Lydiard's reply to the written announcement of Isabel's engagement, despatched on the previous day by Miss Pink.

Her Ladyship's answer was a surprisingly short one. It only contained these lines:

'Lady Lydiard begs to acknowledge the receipt of Miss Pink's letter requesting that she will say nothing to Mr Hardyman of the loss of a bank-note in her house, and, assigning as a reason that Miss Isabel Miller is engaged to be married to Mr Hardyman, and might be prejudiced in his estimation if the facts were made known. Miss Pink may make her mind easy. Lady Lydiard had not the slightest intention of taking Mr Hardyman into her confidence on the subject of her domestic affairs. With regard to the proposed marriage, Lady Lydiard casts no doubt on Miss Pink's perfect sincerity and good faith; but, at the same time, she positively declines to believe that Mr Hardyman means to make Miss Isabel Miller his wife. Lady L. will yield to the evidence of a properly-attested certificate – and to nothing else.'

A folded piece of paper, directed to Isabel, dropped out of this characteristic letter as Miss Pink turned from the first page to the second. Lady Lydiard addressed her adopted daughter in these words:

'I was on the point of leaving home to visit you again, when I received your aunt's letter. My poor deluded child, no words can tell how distressed I am about you. You are already sacrificed to the folly of the most foolish woman living. For God's sake, take care you do not fall a victim next to the designs of a profligate man. Come to me instantly, Isabel, and I promise to take care of you.'

Fortified by these letters, and aided by Miss Pink's indignation, Hardyman pressed his proposal on Isabel with renewed resolution. She made no attempt to combat his arguments – she only held firmly to her decision. Without some encouragement from Hardyman's father and mother, she still steadily refused to become his wife. Irritated already by Lady Lydiard's letters, he lost the self-command which so eminently distinguished him in the ordinary affairs of life, and showed the domineering and despotic temper which was an inbred part of his disposition. Isabel's high spirit at once resented the harsh terms in which he spoke to her. In the plainest words, she released him from his engagement, and, without waiting for his excuses, quitted the room.

Left together, Hardyman and Miss Pink devised an arrangement which paid due respect to Isabel's scruples, and at the same time met Lady Lydiard's insulting assertion of disbelief in Hardyman's honour, by a formal and public announcement of the marriage.

It was proposed to give a garden party at the farm in a week's time, for the express purpose of introducing Isabel to Hardyman's family and friends in the character of his betrothed wife. If his father and mother accepted the invitation, Isabel's only objection to hastening their union would fall to the ground. Hardyman might, in that case, plead with his Imperial correspondent for a delay in his departure of a few days more; and the marriage might still take place before he left England. Isabel, at Miss Pink's intercession, was induced to accept her lover's excuses, and, in the event of her favourable reception by Hardyman's parents at the farm, to give her consent (not very willingly even yet) to hastening the ceremony which was to make her Hardyman's wife.

On the next morning the whole of the invitations were sent out, excepting the invitation to Hardyman's father and mother. Without mentioning it to Isabel, Hardyman decided on personally appealing to his mother before he ventured on taking the head of the family into his confidence.

The result of the interview was partially successful – and no more. Lord Rotherfield declined to see his youngest son; and he had engagements which would, under any circumstances, prevent his being present at the garden party. But, at the express request of Lady Rotherfield, he was willing to make certain concessions.

'I have always regarded Alfred as a barely sane person,' said his Lordship, 'since he turned his back on his prospects to become a horse-dealer. If we decline altogether to sanction this new act – I won't say, of insanity, I will say, of absurdity – on his part, it is impossible to predict to what discreditable extremities he may not proceed. We must temporise with Alfred. In the meantime I shall endeavour to obtain some information respecting this young person – named Miller, I think you said, and now resident at South Morden. If I am satisfied that she is a woman of reputable character, possessing an average education and presentable manners, we may as well let Alfred take his own way. He is out of the pale of Society, as it is; and Miss Miller has no father and mother to complicate matters, which is distinctly a merit on her part – and, in short, if the marriage is not absolutely disgraceful, the wisest way (as we have no power to prevent it) will be to submit. You will say nothing to Alfred about what I propose to do. I tell you plainly I don't trust him. You will simply inform him from me that I want time to consider, and that, unless he hears to the contrary in the interval, he may expect to have the sanction of your presence at his breakfast, or luncheon, or whatever it is. I must go to town in a day or two, and I shall ascertain what Alfred's friends know about this last of his many follies, if I meet any of them at the club.'

Returning to South Morden in no serene frame of mind, Hardyman found Isabel in a state of depression which perplexed and alarmed him.

The news that his mother might be expected to be present at the garden party failed entirely to raise her spirits. The only explanation she gave of the change in her was, that the dull heavy weather of the last few days made her feel a little languid and nervous. Naturally dissatisfied with this reply to his inquiries, Hardyman asked for Miss Pink. He was informed that Miss Pink could not see him. She was constitutionally subject to asthma, and, having warnings of the return of the malady, she was (by the doctor's advice) keeping her room. Hardyman returned to the farm in a temper which was felt by everybody in his employment, from the trainer to the stable-boys.

While the apology made for Miss Pink stated no more than the plain truth, it must be confessed that Hardyman was right in declining to be satisfied with Isabel's excuse for the melancholy that oppressed her. She had that morning received Moody's answer to the lines which she had addressed to him at the end of her aunt's letter; and she had not yet recovered from the effect which it had produced on her spirits.

'It is impossible for me to say honestly that I am not distressed (Moody wrote) by the news of your marriage engagement. The blow has fallen very heavily on me. When I look at the future now, I see only a dreary blank. This is not your fault – you are in no way to blame. I remember the time when I should have been too angry to own this – when I might have said or done things which I should have bitterly repented afterwards. That time is past. My temper has been softened, since I have befriended you in your troubles. That good at least has come out of my foolish hopes, and perhaps out of the true sympathy which I have felt for you. I can honestly ask you to accept my heart's dearest wishes for your happiness – and I can keep the rest to myself.

'Let me say a word now relating to the efforts that I have made to help you, since that sad day when you left Lady Lydiard's house.

'I had hoped (for reasons which it is needless to mention here) to interest Mr Hardyman himself in aiding our inquiry. But your aunt's wishes, as expressed in her letter to me, close my lips. I will only beg you, at some convenient time, to let me mention the last discoveries that we have made; leaving it to your discretion, when Mr Hardyman has become your husband, to ask him the questions which, under other circumstances, I should have put to him myself.

'It is, of course, possible that the view I take of Mr Hardyman's capacity to help us may be a mistaken one. In this case, if you still wish the investigation to be privately carried on, I entreat you to let me continue to direct it, as the greatest favour you can confer on your devoted old friend.

'You need be under no apprehension about the expense to which you are likely to put me. I have unexpectedly inherited what is to me a handsome fortune.

'The same post which brought your aunt's letter brought a line from a lawyer asking me to see him on the subject of my late father's affairs. I waited a day or two before I could summon heart enough to see him, or to see anybody; and then I went to his office. You have heard that my father's bank stopped payment, at a time of commercial panic. His failure was mainly attributable to the treachery of a friend to whom he had lent a large sum of money, and who paid him the yearly interest, without acknowledging that every farthing of it had been lost in unsuccessful speculations. The son of this man has prospered in business, and he has honourably devoted a part of his wealth to the payment of his father's creditors. Half the sum due to *my* father has thus passed into my hands as his next of kin; and the other half is to follow in course of time. If my hopes had been fulfilled, how gladly I should have shared my prosperity with you! As it is, I have far more than enough for my wants as a lonely man, and plenty left to spend in your service.

'God bless and prosper you, my dear. I shall ask you to accept a little present from me, among the other offerings that are made to you before the wedding day. – R.M.'

The studiously considerate and delicate tone in which these lines were written had an effect on Isabel which was exactly the opposite of the effect intended by the writer. She burst into a passionate fit of tears; and in the safe solitude of her own room, the despairing words escaped her, 'I wish I had died before I met with Alfred Hardyman!'

As the days wore on, disappointments and difficulties seemed by a kind of fatality to beset the contemplated announcement of the marriage.

Miss Pink's asthma, developed by the unfavourable weather, set the doctor's art at defiance, and threatened to keep that unfortunate lady a prisoner in her room on the day

of the party. Hardyman's invitations were in some cases
refused; and in others accepted by husbands with excuses for
the absence of their wives. His elder brother made an apology
for himself as well as for his wife. Felix Sweetsir wrote, 'With
pleasure, dear Alfred, if my health permits me to leave the
house.' Lady Lydiard, invited at Miss Pink's special request,
sent no reply. The one encouraging circumstance was the
silence of Lady Rotherfield. So long as her son received no
intimation to the contrary, it was a sign that Lord Rotherfield
permitted his wife to sanction the marriage by her presence.

Hardyman wrote to his Imperial correspondent, engaging
to leave England on the earliest possible day, and asking to be
pardoned if he failed to express himself more definitely, in
consideration of domestic affairs, which it was necessary to
settle before he started for the Continent. If there should not
be time enough to write again, he promised to send a
telegraphic announcement of his departure. Long afterwards,
Hardyman remembered the misgivings that had troubled him
when he wrote that letter. In the rough draught of it, he had
mentioned, as his excuse for not being yet certain of his own
movements, that he expected to be immediately married. In
the fair copy, the vague foreboding of some accident to come
was so painfully present to his mind, that he struck out the
words which referred to his marriage, and substituted the
designedly indefinite phrase, 'domestic affairs.'

CHAPTER XX

The day of the garden party arrived. There was no rain; but
the air was heavy, and the sky was overcast by lowering
clouds.

Some hours before the guests were expected, Isabel arrived
alone at the farm, bearing the apologies of unfortunate Miss
Pink, still kept a prisoner in her bed-chamber by the asthma.
In the confusion produced at the cottage by the preparations
for entertaining the company, the one room in which Hardy-

man could receive Isabel with the certainty of not being interrupted was the smoking-room. To this haven of refuge he led her – still reserved and silent, still not restored to her customary spirits. 'If any visitors come before the time,' Hardyman said to his servant, 'tell them I am engaged at the stables. I must have an hour's quiet talk with you,' he continued, turning to Isabel, 'or I shall be in too bad a temper to receive my guests with common politeness. The worry of giving this party is not to be told in words. I almost wish I had been content with presenting you to my mother, and had let the rest of my acquaintances go to the devil.'

A quiet half hour passed; and the first visitor, a stranger to the servants, appeared at the cottage-gate. He was a middle-aged man, and he had no wish to disturb Mr Hardyman. 'I will wait in the grounds,' he said, 'and trouble nobody.' The middle-aged man, who expressed himself in these modest terms, was Robert Moody.

Five minutes later, a carriage drove up to the gate. An elderly lady got out of it, followed by a fat white Scotch terrier, who growled at ever stranger within his reach. It is needless to introduce Lady Lydiard and Tommie.

Informed that Mr Hardyman was at the stables, Lady Lydiard gave the servant her card. 'Take that to your master, and say I won't detain him five minutes.' With these words, her Ladyship sauntered into the grounds. She looked about her with observant eyes; not only noticing the tent which had been set up on the grass to accommodate the expected guests, but entering it, and looking at the waiters who were engaged in placing the luncheon on the table. Returning to the outer world, she next remarked that Mr Hardyman's lawn was in very bad order. Barren sun-dried patches, and little holes and crevices opened here and there by the action of the summer heat, announced that the lawn, like everything else at the farm, had been neglected, in the exclusive attention paid to the claims of the horses. Reaching a shrubbery which bounded one side of the grounds next, her Ladyship became aware of a man slowly approaching her, to all appearance absorbed in thought. The man drew a little nearer. She lifted her glasses to her eyes and recognized – Moody.

No embarrassment was produced on either side by this unexpected meeting. Lady Lydiard had, not long since, sent to ask her former steward to visit her; regretting, in her warm-hearted way, the terms on which they had separated, and wishing to atone for the harsh language that had escaped her at their parting interview. In the friendly talk which followed the reconciliation, Lady Lydiard not only heard the news of Moody's pecuniary inheritance – but, noticing the change in his appearance for the worse, contrived to extract from him the confession of his ill-starred passion for Isabel. To discover him now, after all that he had acknowledged, walking about the grounds at Hardyman's farm, took her Ladyship completely by surprise. 'Good Heavens!' she exclaimed, in her loudest tones, 'what are you doing here?'

'You mentioned Mr Hardyman's garden party, my Lady, when I had the honour of waiting on you,' Moody answered. 'Thinking over it afterwards, it seemed the fittest occasion I could find for making a little wedding present to Miss Isabel. Is there any harm in my asking Mr Hardyman to let me put the present on her plate, so that she may see it when she sits down to luncheon? If your Ladyship thinks so, I will go away directly, and send the gift by post.'

Lady Lydiard looked at him attentively. 'You don't despise the girl,' she asked, 'for selling herself for rank and money? I do – I can tell you!'

Moody's worn white face flushed a little. 'No, my Lady,' he answered, 'I can't hear you say that! Isabel would not have engaged herself to Mr Hardyman unless she had been fond of him – as fond, I dare say, as I once hoped she might be of me. It's a hard thing to confess that; but I do confess it, in justice to her – God bless her!'

The generosity that spoke in those simple words touched the finest sympathies in Lady Lydiard's nature. 'Give me your hand,' she said, with her own generous spirit kindling in her eyes. 'You have a great heart, Moody. Isabel Miller is a fool for not marrying *you* – and one day she will know it!'

Before a word more could pass between them, Hardyman's voice was audible on the other side of the shrubbery, calling irritably to his servant to find Lady Lydiard.

Moody retired to the farther end of the walk, while Lady Lydiard advanced in the opposite direction, so as to meet Hardyman at the entrance to the shrubbery. He bowed stiffly, and begged to know why her Ladyship had honoured him with a visit.

Lady Lydiard replied without noticing the coldness of her reception.

'I have not been very well, Mr Hardyman, or you would have seen me before this. My only object in presenting myself here is to make my excuses personally for having written of you in terms which expressed a doubt of your honour. I have done you an injustice, and I beg you to forgive me.'

Hardyman acknowledged this frank apology as unreservedly as it had been offered to him. 'Say no more, Lady Lydiard. And let me hope, now you are here, that you will honour my little party with your presence.'

Lady Lydiard gravely stated her reasons for not accepting the invitation.

'I disapprove so strongly of unequal marriages,' she said, walking on slowly towards the cottage, 'that I cannot, in common consistency, become one of your guests. I shall always feel interested in Isabel Miller's welfare; and I can honestly say I shall be glad if your married life proves that my old-fashioned prejudices are without justification in your case. Accept my thanks for your invitation; and let me hope that my plain-speaking has not offended you.'

She bowed, and looked about her for Tommie before she advanced to the carriage waiting for her at the gate. In the surprise of seeing Moody she had forgotten to look back for the dog when she entered the shrubbery. She now called to him, and blew the whistle at her watch-chain. Not a sign of Tommie was to be seen. Hardyman instantly directed the servants to search in the cottage and out of the cottage for the dog. The order was obeyed with all needful activity and intelligence, and entirely without success. For the time being, at any rate, Tommie was lost.

Hardyman promised to have the dog looked for in every part of the farm, and to send him back in the care of one of his own men. With these polite assurances Lady Lydiard was obliged to be satisfied. She drove away in a very despondent frame of mind. 'First Isabel, and now Tommie,' thought her Ladyship. 'I am losing the only companions who made life tolerable to me.'

Returning from the garden gate, after taking leave of his visitor, Hardyman received from his servant a handful of letters which had just arrived for him. Walking slowly over the lawn as he opened them, he found nothing but excuses for the absence of guests who had already accepted their invitations. He had just thrust the letters into his pocket, when he heard footsteps behind him, and, looking round, found himself confronted by Moody.

'Hullo! have you come to lunch?' Hardyman asked roughly.

'I have come here, sir, with a little gift for Miss Isabel, in honour of her marriage,' Moody answered quietly. 'And I ask your permission to put it on the table, so that she may see it when your guests sit down to luncheon.'

He opened a jeweller's case as he spoke, containing a plain gold bracelet with an inscription engraved on the inner side: – 'To Miss Isabel Miller, with the sincere good wishes of Robert Moody.'

Plain as it was, the design of the bracelet was unusually beautiful. Hardyman had noticed Moody's agitation on the day when he had met Isabel near her aunt's house, and had drawn his own conclusions from it. His face darkened with a momentary jealousy as he looked at the bracelet. 'All right, old fellow!' he said, with contemptuous familiarity. 'Don't be modest. Wait and give it to her with your own hand.'

'No, sir,' said Moody 'I would rather leave it, if you please, to speak for itself.'

Hardyman understood the delicacy of feeling which dictated those words, and, without well knowing why, resented it. He was on the point of speaking, under the influence of this unworthy motive, when Isabel's voice reached his ears, calling to him from the cottage.

Moody's face contracted with a sudden expression of pain as he too recognised the voice. 'Don't let me detain you, sir,' he said sadly. 'Good morning!'

Hardyman left him without ceremony. Moody, slowly following, entered the tent. All the preparations for the luncheon had been completed; nobody was there. The places to be occupied by the guests were indicated by cards bearing their names. Moody found Isabel's card, and put his bracelet inside the folded napkin on her plate. For a while he stood with his hand on the table, thinking. The temptation to communicate once more with Isabel before he lost her for ever, was fast getting the better of his powers of resistance. 'If I could persuade her to write a word to say she liked her bracelet,' he thought, 'it would be a comfort when I go back to my solitary life.' He tore a leaf out of his pocket book and wrote on it, 'One line to say you accept my gift and my good wishes. Put it under the cushion of your chair, and I shall find it when the company have left the tent.' He slipped the paper into the case which held the bracelet, and instead of leaving the farm as he had intended, turned back to the shelter of the shrubbery.

CHAPTER XXI

Hardyman went on to the cottage. He found Isabel in some agitation. And there, by her side, with his tail wagging slowly, and his eye on Hardyman in expectation of a possible kick – there was the lost Tommie!

'Has Lady Lydiard gone?' Isabel asked eagerly.

'Yes,' said Hardyman. 'Where did you find the dog?'

As events had ordered it, the dog had found Isabel, under these circumstances.

The appearance of Lady Lydiard's card in the smoking-room had been an alarming event for Lady Lydiard's adopted daughter. She was guiltily conscious of not having answered her Ladyship's note, enclosed in Miss Pink's letter, and of not having taken her Ladyship's advice in regulating her conduct towards Hardyman. As he rose to leave the room and receive his visitor in the grounds, Isabel begged him to say nothing of her presence at the farm, unless Lady Lydiard exhibited a forgiving turn of mind by asking to see her. Left by herself in the smoking-room, she suddenly heard a bark in the passage which had a familiar sound in her ears. She opened the door – and in rushed Tommie, with one of his shrieks of delight! Curiosity had taken him into the house. He had heard the voices in the smoking-room; had recognized Isabel's voice; and had waited, with his customary cunning and his customary distrust of strangers, until Hardyman was out of the way. Isabel kissed and caressed him, and then drove him out again to the lawn, fearing that Lady Lydiard might return to look for him. Going back to the smoking-room, she stood at the window watching for Hardyman's return. When the servants came to look for the dog, she could only tell them that she had last seen him in the grounds, not far from cottage. The useless search being abandoned, and the carriage having left the gate, who should crawl out from the back of a cupboard in which some empty hampers were placed but Tommie himself! How he had contrived to get back to the smoking-room (unless she had omitted to completely close the door on her return) it was impossible to say. But there he was, determined this time to stay with Isabel, and keeping in his hiding place until he heard the movement of the carriage-wheels, which informed him that his lawful mistress had left the cottage! Isabel had at once called Hardyman, on the chance that the carriage might yet be stopped. It was already out of sight, and nobody knew which of two roads it had taken, both leading to London. In this emergency, Isabel could only look at Hardyman and ask what was to be done.

'I can't spare a servant till after the party,' he answered. 'The dog must be tied up in the stables.'

Isabel shook her head. Tommie was not accustomed to be tied up. He would make a disturbance, and he would be beaten by the grooms. 'I will take care of him,' she said. 'He won't leave me.'

'There's something else to think of besides the dog,' Hardyman rejoined irritably. 'Look at these letters!' He pulled them out of his pocket as he spoke. 'Here are no less than seven men, all calling themselves my friends, who accepted my invitation, and who write to excuse themselves on the very day of the party. Do you know why? They're all afraid of my father – I forgot to tell you he's a Cabinet Minister as well as a Lord. Cowards and cads. They have heard he isn't coming, and they think to curry favour with the great man by stopping away. Come along, Isabel! Let's take their names off the luncheon table. Not a man of them shall ever darken my doors again!'

'I am to blame for what has happened,' Isabel answered sadly. 'I am estranging you from your friends. There is still time, Alfred, to alter your mind and let me go.'

He put his arm round her with rough fondness. 'I would sacrifice every friend I have in the world rather than lose you. Come along!'

They left the cottage. At the entrance to the tent, Hardyman noticed the dog at Isabel's heels, and vented his ill-temper, as usual with male humanity, on the nearest unoffending creature that he could find 'Be off, you mongrel brute!' he shouted. The tail of Tommie relaxed from its customary tight curve over the small of his back; and the legs of Tommie (with his tail between them) took him at full gallop to the friendly shelter of the cupboard in the smoking-room. It was one of those trifling circumstances which women notice seriously. Isabel said nothing; she only thought to herself, 'I wish he had shown his temper when I first knew him!'

They entered the tent.

'I'll read the names,' said Hardyman, 'and you find the cards and tear them up. Stop! I'll keep the cards. You're just the sort of woman my father likes. He'll be reconciled to me when he sees you, after we are married. If one of those men ever asks him for a place, I'll take care, if it's years hence, to put an obstacle in his way! Here, take my pencil, and make a mark on the cards to remind me; – the same mark I set against a horse in my book when I don't like him – a cross, enclosed in a circle.' He produced his pocket-book. His hands trembled with anger as he gave the pencil to Isabel and laid the book on the table. He had just read the name of the first false friend, and Isabel had just found the card, when a servant appeared with a message. 'Mrs Drumblade has arrived, sir, and wishes to see you on a matter of the greatest importance.'

Hardyman left the tent, not very willingly. 'Wait here,' he said to Isabel; 'I'll be back directly.'

She was standing near her own place at the table. Moody had left one end of the jeweller's case visible above the napkin, to attract her attention. In a minute more the bracelet and note were in her hands. She dropped on her chair, overwhelmed by the conflicting emotions that rose in her at the sight of the bracelet, at the reading of the note. Her head drooped, and the tears filled her eyes. 'Are all women as blind as I have been to what is good and noble in the men who love them?' she wondered, sadly. 'Better as it is,' she thought, with a bitter sigh; 'I am not worthy of him.'

As she took up the pencil to write her answer to Moody on the back of her dinner-card, the servant appeared again at the door of the tent.

'My master wants you at the cottage, Miss, immediately.'

Isobel rose, putting the bracelet and the note in the silver-mounted leather pocket (a present from Hardyman) which hung at her belt. In the hurry of passing round the table to get out, she never noticed that her dress touched Hardyman's pocket-book, placed close to the edge, and threw it down on the grass below. The book fell into one of the heat-cracks which Lady Lydiard had noticed as evidence of the neglected condition of the cottage lawn.

'You ought to hear the pleasant news my sister has just brought me,' said Hardyman, when Isabel joined him in the parlour. 'Mrs Drumblade has been told, on the best authority, that my mother is not coming to the party.'

'There must be some reason, of course, dear Isabel,' added Mrs Drumblade. 'Have you any idea of what it can be? I haven't seen my mother myself; and all my inquiries have failed to find it out.'

She looked searchingly at Isabel as she spoke. The mask of sympathy on her face was admirably worn. Nobody who possessed only a superficial acquaintance with Mrs Drumblade's character would have suspected how thoroughly she was enjoying in secret the position of embarrassment in which her news had placed her brother. Instinctively doubting whether Mrs Drumblade's friendly behaviour was quite as sincere as it appeared to be, Isabel answered that she was a stranger to Lady Rotherfield, and was therefore quite at a loss to explain the cause of her ladyship's absence. As she spoke, the guests began to arrive in quick succession, and the subject was dropped as a matter of course.

It was not a merry party. Hardyman's approaching marriage had been made the topic of much malicious gossip; and Isabel's character had, as usual in such cases, become the object of all the false reports that scandal could invent. Lady Rotherfield's absence confirmed the general conviction that Hardyman was disgracing himself. The men were all more or less uneasy. The women resented the discovery that Isabel was – personally speaking, at least – beyond the reach of hostile criticism. Her beauty was viewed as a downright offence; her refined and modest manners were set down as perfect acting; 'really disgusting, my dear, in so young a girl.' General Drumblade, a large and mouldy veteran, in a state of chronic astonishment (after his own matrimonial experience) at Hardyman's folly in marrying at all, diffused a wide circle of gloom, wherever he went and whatever he did. His accomplished wife, forcing her high spirits on everybody's attention with a sort of kittenish playfulness, intensified the depressing effect of the general dullness by all the force of the strongest contrast. After waiting half an hour for his mother, and waiting in vain, Hardyman led the way to the tent in despair. 'The sooner I fill their stomachs and get rid of them,' he thought savagely, 'the better I shall be pleased!'

The luncheon was attacked by the company with a certain silent ferocity, which the waiters noticed as remarkable, even in their large experience The men drank deeply, but with wonderfully little effect in raising their spirits; the women, with the exception of amiable Mrs Drumblade, kept Isabel deliberately out of the conversation that went on among them. General Drumblade, sitting next to her in one of the places of honour, discoursed to Isabel privately on 'my brother-in-law Hardyman's infernal temper'. A young marquis, on her other side – a mere lad, chosen to make the necessary speech in acknowledgment of his superior rank – rose, in a state of nervous trepidation, to propose Isabel's health as the chosen bride of their host. Pale and trembling, conscious of having forgotten the words which he had learnt before-hand, this unhappy young nobleman began, 'Ladies and gentlemen, I haven't an idea —— ' He stopped, put his hand to his head, stared wildly, and sat down again; having contrived to state his own case with masterly brevity and perfect truth, in a speech of seven words.

While the dismay, in some cases, and the amusement in others, was still at its height, Hardyman's valet made his appearance, and, approaching his master, said in a whisper, 'Could I speak to you, sir, for a moment outside?'

'What the devil do you want?' Hardyman asked irritably. 'Is that a letter in your hand? Give it to me.'

The valet was a Frenchman. In other words, he had a sense of what was due to himself. His master had forgotten this. He gave up the letter with a certain dignity of manner, and left the tent. Hardyman opened the letter. He turned pale as he read it; crumpled it in his hand, and threw it down on the table. 'By G——d! it's a lie!' he exclaimed furiously.

The guests rose in confusion. Mrs Drumblade, finding the letter within her reach, coolly possessed herself of it; recognized her mother's handwriting; and read these lines:

'I have only now succeeded in persuading your father to let me write to you. For God's sake, break off your marriage at any sacrifice. Your father has heard, on unanswerable authority, that Miss Isabel Miller left her situation in Lady Lydiard's house on suspicion of theft.'

While his sister was reading this letter, Hardyman had made his way to Isabel's chair. 'I must speak to you, directly,' he whispered. 'Come away with me!' He turned, as he took her arm, and looked at the table. 'Where is my letter?' he asked. Mrs Drumblade handed it to him, dexterously crumpled up again as she had found it. 'No bad news, dear Alfred, I hope?' she said, in her most affectionate manner. Hardyman snatched the letter from her, without answering, and led Isabel out of the tent.

'Read that!' he said, when they were alone. 'And tell me at once whether it's true or false.'

Isabel read the letter. For a moment the shock of the discovery held her speechless. She recovered herself, and returned the letter.

'It is true,' she answered.

Hardyman staggered back as if she had shot him.

'True that you are guilty?' he asked.

'No; I am innocent. Everybody who knows me believes in my innocence. It is true the appearances were against me. They are against me still.' Having said this, she waited, quietly and firmly, for his next words.

He passed his hand over his forehead with a sigh of relief.

'It's bad enough as it is,' he said, speaking quietly on his side.
'But the remedy for it is plain enough. Come back to the tent.'

She never moved. 'Why?' she asked.

'Do you suppose I don't believe in your innocence too?' he
answered. 'The one way of setting you right with the world
now is for me to make you my wife, in spite of the appearances
that point to you. I'm too fond of you, Isabel, to give you up.
Come back with me, and I will announce our marriage to my
friends.'

She took his hand, and kissed it. 'It is generous and good of
you,' she said; 'but it must not be.'

He took a step nearer to her. 'What do you mean?' he asked.

'It was against my will,' she pursued, 'that my aunt
concealed the truth from you. I did wrong to consent to it; I
will do wrong no more. Your mother is right, Alfred. After
what has happened, I am not fit to be your wife until my
innocence is proved. It is not proved yet.'

The angry colour began to rise in his face once more. 'Take
care,' he said; 'I am not in a humour to be trifled with.'

'I am not trifling with you,' she answered, in low, sad tones.

'You really mean what you say?'

'I mean it.'

'Don't be obstinate, Isabel. Take time to consider.'

'You are very kind, Alfred. My duty is plain to me. I will
marry you – if you still wish it – when my good name is
restored to me. Not before.'

He laid one hand on her arm, and pointed with the other to
the guests in the distance, all leaving the tent on the way to their
carriages.

'Your good name will be restored to you,' he said, 'on the
day when I make you my wife. The worst enemy you have
cannot associate *my* name with a suspicion of theft. Remember
that and think a little before you decide. You see those people
there. If you don't change your mind by the time they have got
to the cottage, it's good-bye between us, and good-bye for
ever. I refuse to wait for you; I refuse to accept a conditional
engagement. Wait, and think. They're walking slowly; you
have got some minutes more.'

He still held her arm, watching the guests as they gradually
receded from view. It was not until they had all collected in a

group outside the cottage door that he spoke himself, or that he permitted Isabel to speak again.

'Now,' he said, 'you have had your time to get cool. Will you take my arm, and join those people with me? or will you say good-by for ever?'

'Forgive me, Alfred!' she began, gently. 'I cannot consent, in justice to you, to shelter myself behind your name. It is the name of your family; and they have a right to expect that you will not degrade it —— '

'I want a plain answer,' he interposed sternly. 'Which is it? Yes, or No?'

She looked at him with sad compassionate eyes. Her voice was firm as she answered him in one word as he had desired. The word was – 'No.'

Without speaking to her, without even looking at her, he turned and walked back to the cottage.

Making his way silently through the group of visitors – every one of whom had been informed of what had happened by his sister – with his head down and his lips fast closed, he entered the parlour, and rang the bell which communicated with his foreman's rooms at the stables.

'You know that I am going abroad on business?' he said, when the man appeared.

'Yes, sir.'

'I am going to-day – going by the night train to Dover. Order the horse to be put to instantly in the dog-cart. Is there anything wanted before I am off?'

The inexorable necessities of business asserted their claims through the obedient medium of the foreman. Chafing at the delay, Hardyman was obliged to sit at his desk, signing cheques and passing accounts, with the dog-cart waiting in the stable-yard.

A knock at the door startled him in the middle of his work. 'Come in,' he called out sharply.

He looked up, expecting to see one of the guests or one of the servants. It was Moody who entered the room. Hardyman laid down his pen, and fixed his eyes sternly on the man who had dared to interrupt him.

'What the devil do *you* want?' he asked.

'I have seen Miss Isabel, and spoken with her,' Moody

replied. 'Mr Hardyman, I believe it is in your power to set this matter right. For the young lady's sake, sir, you must not leave England without doing it.'

Hardyman turned to his foreman. 'Is this fellow mad or drunk?' he asked.

Moody proceeded as calmly and as resolutely as if those words had not been spoken. 'I apologize for my intrusion, sir. I will trouble you with no explanations. I will only ask one question. Have you a memorandum of the number of that five-hundred pound note you paid away in France?'

Hardyman lost all control over himself.

'You scoundrel!' he cried, 'have you been prying into my private affairs? Is it *your* business to know what I did in France?'

'Is it *your* vengeance on a woman to refuse to tell her the number of a bank-note?' Moody rejoined, firmly.

That answer forced its way, through Hardyman's anger, to Hardyman's sense of honour. He rose and advanced to Moody. For a moment the two men faced each other in silence. 'You're a bold fellow,' said Hardyman, with a sudden change from anger to irony. 'I'll do the lady justice. I'll look at my pocket-book.'

He put his hand into the breast-pocket of his coat; he searched his other pockets; he turned over the objects on his writing-table. The book was gone.

Moody watched him with a feeling of despair. 'Oh! Mr Hardyman, don't say you have lost your pocket-book!'

He sat down again at his desk, with sullen submission to the new disaster. 'All I can say is you're at liberty to look for it,' he replied. 'I must have dropped it somewhere.' He turned impatiently to the foreman, 'Now then! What is the next cheque wanted? I shall go mad if I wait in this damned place much longer!'

Moody left him, and found his way to the servants' offices. 'Mr Hardyman has lost his pocket-book,' he said. 'Look for it, indoors and out – on the lawn, and in the tent. Ten pounds reward for the man who finds it!'

Servants and waiters instantly dispersed, eager for the promised reward. The men who pursued the search outside the cottage divided their forces. Some of them examined the lawn and the flower-beds. Others went straight to the empty tent. These last were too completely absorbed in pursuing the object in view to notice that they disturbed a dog, eating a stolen lunch of his own from the morsels left on the plates. The dog slunk away under the canvas when the men came in, waited in hiding until they had gone, then returned to the tent, and went on with his luncheon.

Moody hastened back to the part of the grounds (close to the shrubbery) in which Isabel was waiting his return.

She looked at him, while he was telling her of his interview with Hardyman, with an expression in her eyes which he had never seen in them before – an expression which set his heart beating wildly, and made him break off in his narrative before he had reached the end.

'I understand,' she said quietly, as he stopped in confusion. 'You have made one more sacrifice to my welfare. Robert! I believe you are the noblest man that ever breathed the breath of life!'

His eyes sank before hers; he blushed like a boy. 'I have done nothing for you yet,' he said. 'Don't despair of the future, if the pocket-book should not be found. I know who the man is who received the bank-note; and I have only to find him to decide the question whether it *is* the stolen note or not.'

She smiled sadly as his enthusiasm. 'Are you going back to Mr Sharon to help you?' she asked. 'That trick he played me has destroyed *my* belief in him. He no more knows than I do who the thief really is.'

'You are mistaken, Isabel. He knows – and I know.' He stopped there, and made a sign to her to be silent. One of the servants was approaching them.

'Is the pocket-book found?' Moody asked.

'No, sir.'

'Has Mr Hardyman left the cottage?'

'He has just gone, sir. Have you any further instructions to give us?'

'No. There is my address in London, if the pocket-book should be found.'

The man took the card that was handed to him and retired. Moody offered his arm to Isabel. 'I am at your service,' he said, 'when you wish to return to your aunt.'

They had advanced nearly as far as the tent, on their way out of the grounds, when they were met by a gentleman walking towards them from the cottage. He was a stranger to Isabel. Moody immediately recognised him as Mr Felix Sweetsir.

'Ha! our good Moody!' cried Felix. 'Enviable man! you look younger than ever.' He took off his hat to Isabel; his bright restless eyes suddenly became quiet as they rested on her. 'Have I the honour of addressing the future Mrs Hardyman? May I offer my best congratulations? What has become of our friend Alfred?'

Moody answered for Isabel. 'If you will make inquiries at the cottage, sir,' he said, 'you will find that you are mistaken, to say the least of it, in addressing your questions to this young lady.'

Felix took off his hat again — with the most becoming appearance of surprise and distress.

'Something wrong, I fear?' he said, addressing Isabel. 'I am, indeed, ashamed if I have ignorantly given you a moment's pain. Pray accept my most sincere apologies. I have only this instant arrived; my health would not allow me to be present at the luncheon. Permit me to express the earnest hope that matters may be set right to the satisfaction of all parties. Good afternoon!'

He bowed with elaborate courtesy, and turned back to the cottage.

'Who is that?' Isabel asked.

'Lady Lydiard's nephew, Mr Felix Sweetsir,' Moody answered, with a sudden sternness of tone, and a sudden coldness of manner, which surprised Isabel.

'You don't like him?' she said.

As she spoke, Felix stopped to give audience to one of the grooms, who had apparently been sent with a message to him. He turned so that his face was once more visible to Isabel. Moody pressed her hand significantly as it rested on his arm.

'Look well at that man,' he whispered. 'It's time to warn you. Mr Felix Sweetsir is the worst enemy you have!'

Isabel heard him in speechless astonishment. He went on in tones that trembled with suppressed emotion.

'You doubt if Sharon knows the thief. You doubt if I know

the thief. Isabel! as certainly as the heaven is above us, there stands the wretch who stole the bank-note!'

She drew her hand out of his arm with a cry of terror. She looked at him as if she doubted whether he was in his right mind.

He took her hand, and waited a moment trying to compose himself.

'Listen to me,' he said. 'At the first consultation I had with Sharon he gave this advice to Mr Troy and to me. He said, "Suspect the very last person on whom suspicion could possibly fall." Those words, taken with the questions he had asked before he pronounced his opinion, struck through me as if he had struck me with a knife. I instantly suspected Lady Lydiard's nephew. Wait! From that time to this I have said nothing of my suspicion to any living soul. I knew in my own heart that it took its rise in the inveterate dislike that I have always felt for Mr Sweetsir, and I distrusted it accordingly. But I went back to Sharon, for all that, and put the case into his hands. His investigations informed me that Mr Sweetsir owed "debts of honour" (as gentlemen call them), incurred through lost bets, to a large number of persons, and among them a bet of five hundred pounds lost to Mr Hardyman. Further inquiries showed that Mr Hardyman had taken the lead in declaring that he would post Mr Sweetsir as a defaulter, and have him turned out of his clubs, and turned out of the betting-ring. Ruin stared him in the face if he failed to pay his debt to Mr Hardyman on the last day left to him – the day after the note was lost. On that very morning, Lady Lydiard, speaking to me of her nephew's visit to her, said, "If I had given him an opportunity of speaking, Felix would have borrowed money of me; I saw it in his face." One moment more, Isabel. I am not only certain that Mr Sweetsir took the five-hundred pound note out of the open letter, I am firmly persuaded that he is the man who told Lord Rotherfield of the circumstances under which you left Lady Lydiard's house. Your marriage to Mr Hardyman might have put you in a position to detect the theft. You, not I, might, in that case, have discovered from your husband that the stolen note was the note with which Mr Sweetsir paid his debt. He came here, you may depend on it, to make sure that he had succeeded in destroying your prospects. A more depraved villain at heart than that man never swung from a gallows!'

He checked himself at those words. The shock of the disclosure, the passion and vehemence with which he spoke, over-whelmed Isabel. She trembled like a frightened child.

While he was still trying to soothe and reassure her, a low whining made itself heard at her feet. They looked down, and saw Tommie. Finding himself noticed at last, he expressed his sense of relief by a bark. Something dropped out of his mouth. As Moody stooped to pick it up, the dog ran to Isabel and pushed his head against her feet, as his way was when he expected to have the handkerchief thrown over him, preparatory to one of those games at hide-and-seek which have been already mentioned. Isabel put out her hand to caress him, when she was stopped by a cry from Moody. It was *his* turn to tremble now. His voice faltered as he said the words, 'The dog has found the pocket-book!'

He opened the book with shaking hands. A betting-book was bound up in it, with the customary calendar. He turned to the date of the day after the robbery.

There was the entry: – 'Felix Sweetsir. Paid £500. Note numbered, N 8, 70564; dated 15 May, 1875.'

Moody took from his waistcoat-pocket his own memorandum of the number of the lost bank-note. 'Read it, Isabel,' he said. 'I won't trust my memory.'

She read it. The number and date of the note entered in the pocket-book exactly corresponded with the number and date of the note that Lady Lydiard had placed in her letter.

Moody handed the pocket-book to Isabel. 'There is the proof of your innocence,' he said, 'thanks to the dog! Will you write and tell Mr Hardyman what has happened?' he asked, with his head down, and his eyes on the ground.

She answered him, with the bright colour suddenly flowing over her face.

'*You* shall write to him,' she said, 'when the time comes.'

'What time?' he asked.

She threw her arms round his neck, and hid her face on his bosom.

'The time,' she whispered, 'when I am your wife.'

A low growl from Tommie reminded them that he too had some claim to be noticed.

Isabel dropped on her knees, and saluted her old playfellow with the heartiest kisses she had ever given him since the day when their acquaintance began. 'You darling!' she said, as she put him down again, 'what can I do to reward you?'

Tommie rolled over on his back – more slowly than usual, in consequence of his luncheon in the tent. He elevated his four paws in the air, and looked lazily at Isabel out of his bright brown eyes. If ever a dog's look spoke yet, Tommie's look said, 'I have eaten too much; rub my stomach.'

POSTSCRIPT

Persons of a speculative turn of mind are informed that the following document is for sale, and are requested to mention what sum they will give for it.

'IOU, Lady Lydiard, five hundred pounds (£500), Felix Sweetsir.'

Her Ladyship became possessed of this pecuniary remittance under circumstances which surround it with a halo of romantic interest. It was the last communication she was destined to receive from her accomplished nephew. There was a Note attached to it, which cannot fail to enhance its value in the estimation of all right-minded persons who assist the circulation of paper money.

The lines that follow are strictly confidential:

'Note. – Our excellent Moody informs me, my dear aunt, that you have decided (against his advice) on "refusing to prosecute". I have not the slightest idea of what he means; but I am very much obliged to him, nevertheless, for reminding me of a circumstance which is of some interest to yourself personally.

'I am on the point of retiring to the Continent in search of health. One generally forgets something important when one starts on a journey. Before Moody called, I had entirely forgotten to mention that I had the pleasure of borrowing five hundred pounds of you some little time since.

'On the occasion to which I refer, your language and manner suggested that you would not lend me the money if I asked for it. Obviously, the only course left was to take it without asking. I took it while Moody was gone to get some curaçoa; and I returned to the picture-gallery in time to receive that delicious liqueur from the footman's hands.

'You will naturally ask why I found it necessary to supply myself (if I may borrow an expression from the language of State finance) with this "forced loan". I was actuated by motives which I think do me honour. My position at the time was critical in the extreme. My credit with the money-lenders was at an end; my friends had all turned their backs on me. I must either take the money or disgrace my family. If there is a man living who is sincerely attached to his family, I am that man. I took the money.

'Conceive your position as my aunt (I say nothing of myself), if I had adopted the other alternative. Turned out of the Jockey Club, turned out of Tattersalls', turned out of the betting-ring; in short, posted publicly as a defaulter before the noblest institution in England, the Turf – and all for want of five hundred pounds to stop the mouth of the greatest brute I know of, Alfred Hardyman! Let me not harrow your feelings (and mine) by dwelling on it. Dear and admirable woman! To you belongs the honour of saving the credit of the family; I can claim nothing but the inferior merit of having offered you the opportunity.

'My I O U, it is needless to say, accompanies these lines. Can I do anything for you abroad? – F.S.'

To this it is only necessary to add (first) that Moody was perfectly right in believing F.S. to be the person who informed Hardyman's father of Isabel's position when she left Lady Lydiard's house; and (secondly) that Felix did really forward Mr Troy's narrative of the theft to the French police, altering nothing in it but the number of the lost bank-note.

What is there left to write about? Nothing is left – but to say good-bye (very sorrowfully on the writer's part) to the Persons of the Story.

Good-bye to Miss Pink —— who will regret to her dying day that Isabel's answer to Hardyman was No.

Good-bye to Lady Lydiard – who differs with Miss Pink, and would have regretted it, to *her* dying day, if the answer had been Yes.

Good-bye to Moody and Isabel – whose history has closed with the closing of the clergyman's book on their wedding-day.

Good-bye to Hardyman – who has sold his farm and his horses, and has begun a new life among the famous fast trotters of America.

Good-bye to Old Sharon – who, a martyr to his promise, brushed his hair and washed his face in honour of Moody's marriage; and catching a severe cold as the necessary consequence, declared, in the intervals of sneezing, that he would 'never do it again'.

And last, not least, good-bye to Tommie? No. The writer gave Tommie his dinner not half an hour since, and is too fond of him to say good-bye.

THE END

VICTOR HUGO

THE TOILERS
OF THE SEA

Following Mess Lethierry's decision to set up a ferry service between Guernsey and St Malo, on the French coast, there is much hostility to the first steam vessel in the Channel, but critics are confounded by its success. When the mysterious Sieur Clubin takes over as captain, however, the dangerous adventures that lie ahead begin to unfold, and it is not long before the momentous role that the novel's hero, Gilliat, must play is made clear.

In this dramatic tale of adventure, intrigue, humour and romance, Victor Hugo once again displays his natural gifts as masterful story-teller, taking as his setting the island of Guernsey (where he lived for fifteen years) in the years after the French Revolution. Dedicated to all 'toilers of the sea', be they fishermen, sailors, ferrymen or smugglers, this exhilarating novel became an unprecedented best seller on its first publication in 1866, and caused a sensation second only to that achieved by *Les Misérables* four years earlier.

CHARLES DICKENS
AND
WILKIE COLLINS

NO THOROUGHFARE
& Other Stories

When Walter Wilding the London wine-merchant discovers the true significance of his name from an unexpected source, he sets out to uncover and put to rights the confusion which occurred at the foundling hospital of his childhood. That 'No Thoroughfare' seems possible indicates only the beginning of a story of adventure and romance which sets the tone for an exciting collection that ranges from the comic festivities of 'The Blooms-bury Christening' to the tense 'Hunted Down', based on the character of a real-life forger and poisoner. Moreover, many of these stories, including the 'Lazy Tour of Two Idle Appren-tices', which (along with 'No Thoroughfare') was written in collaboration with his friend Wilkie Collins, become almost confessional in their auto-biographical revelations of Dickens's private life.

CHARLES DICKENS

THE SIGNALMAN
& Other Ghost Stories

In the title story, a ghostly apparition warns of impending doom on a desolate stretch of railway track. 'The Haunted Man' is an unhappy wretch – his voice and manner are those of a man beset with supernatural troubles, and his lair, part library and part laboratory, is solitary and vault-like: what secrets does it conceal? A moral lesson is taught to Gabriel Grub the gravedigger in 'The Story of the Goblins who Stole a Sexton', and in 'The Hanged Man's Bride' a young girl, taken to live in a fortune-hunter's house, is willed to die; but her murderer lives on – even after his crime has been paid for. . . .

Charles Dickens would entertain and alarm guests at his soirées with his imaginary creations. This collection of stories, to be read at dusk in flickering firelight, brings together many of his spine-chilling masterpieces: these are fifteen tales which will remain in the mind long after the book is back on the shelf.

WILKIE COLLINS

MAN AND WIFE

The daughter of a woman unjustifiably cast aside by her mulish husband and facing social disgrace when he contrives to announce their marriage invalid on a point of ceremony, Anne Silvester is taken into the household of her mother's childhood friend, Lady Lundie. Blanche, Lady Lundie's sweet-natured daughter, becomes inseparable from Anne – as their mothers were many years before. When Anne falls in love with manipulative social climber Geoffrey Delamayn it seems as if she is about to relive her mother's mistakes. Manoeuvred into an intolerable situation by the heartless Geoffrey, whose interests lie only in himself as an aspiring athlete and in the acquisition of money, Anne flees – to find that her honourable actions avail her nothing. . . .

Two main themes occupy Wilkie Collins in this novel of social mores: the inequality of the marriage laws and the spread of brutality among 'gentlemen' who practice violent and self-aggrandizing sports. In what is perhaps his most outspoken work he offers a treatise on the social problems rife among his contemporaries and an exposée of the myths of social status.